New Age

D1522679

Woodstock to St. Joseph's

by

Steve Lindahl

Publisher's Note:

This is a work of fiction. All names, characters, places, and events are the work of the author's imagination.

Any resemblance to real persons, places, or events is coincidental.

Solstice Publishing - http://www.solsticeempire.com/

As my editor began working on this novel, I learned of the passing of one of my best friends, Robert W. Gates, whom I had known since we were teenagers.

I have countless memories of the times I shared with him. Among the best of those is the time we spent at the 1969 Woodstock Festival.

I would like to dedicate this book to Bob Gates and to the others who were with us:
Kevin Brady, Gene Dillman, Don Hancock, Sutushti Lang, Bruce Langenkamp, Jim Lent, Mike Manning, and Jack Moore.

St. Joseph's Oratory
On the Steps #1

Nothing less than the hand of God could cure Gregory's cancer, so Corinne brought her father on a journey from his home in Saugerties, NY in search of a miracle.

Corinne and Gregory prayed, then leaned forward and kissed the step. They were side by side, almost as close to each other as they would have been had she touched her lips to his forehead. Instead, they kissed a plank of wood, one that had been walked on, crawled over, and kissed by thousands of other pilgrims. This was the first stair leading up to St. Joseph's Oratory in Montreal, Quebec. They were on their way but there were ninety-nine steps in total. This was still the beginning even if you counted the nearly two hundred seventy-five miles they'd driven to get to this basilica.

Gregory didn't look good and he knew it. Due to the chemotherapy he was thin, on the edge of skinny, and he'd lost about all his hair. He was fifty-five but felt more like eighty-five. Back when his wife was alive, when he was in his twenties and healthy, he wasn't bad looking. His waist was a bit too big, mostly due to his love handles, and his thick head of hair had started to thin. But he kept hints of his old widow's peak until the drugs did their damage. His upper body had once been strong and he had nice features, especially his dark eyes which were deep-set with long lashes. His skin had always been ruddy even in the winter when he spent most of his time indoors. Gregory was an average height but he hadn't minded because back then his five-foot-nine could hold his wife's five-foot-seven as well as the sky held the stars.

They moved to the second step and kissed it.

Gregory stopped attending any religious services a year after the accident, even Easter and Christmas, and he didn't go back until Corinne heard her mom's voice in the windchimes. He blamed God for his wife's death but told his young daughter he left the church for a different reason. He said he objected to the church's opposition to birth control, which was rigidly adhered to back then. "Unwanted babies change everything."

"Did you want *me*?" she asked him.

He felt his mouth go dry. "You were our greatest blessing."

Corinne did not blame God for her mother's death. She was too busy blaming herself. When she was fourteen God reached out to her, which was when she began attending church.

She became a protestant but not because her father decided to leave the Catholic church. A Methodist church called to her. Despite Corinne's early protestant allegiance, Catholicism seemed to be in her genes. Later in life she attended an Episcopalian church (the church describes itself as 'Protestant, yet Catholic') and eventually her need for Catholic miracles led her to Brother André and St. Joseph's Oratory.

The miracles at St. Joseph's Oratory started with Brother André, a quiet, humble man who worked at Notre Dame Basilica in Montreal during the late nineteenth and early twentieth centuries.

The first miracle occurred in an infirmary when Brother André told a boy who had been running a fever he was not sick and should go out and play with his friends. The doctors were amazed Brother André was right and the fever was gone, but they did not credit him with the power to heal, not until other miracles occurred.

The main doctor at Notre Dame was convinced Brother André was a fraud until the doctor's wife started hemorrhaging blood from her nose. That doctor could do nothing to help her nor could any of his colleagues. The woman begged her husband to call in Brother André. The doctor loved his wife and finally gave in to her pleas. As soon as Brother André walked into her room the bleeding stopped.

There were other miraculous cures of smashed limbs and broken spines and burned faces during Brother André's lifetime, and as more and more influential people were convinced, Brother André was able to raise the funds to build the beautiful structure standing there today.

He never took credit for those miracles, instead he attributed them to St. Joseph, and after Brother André died they continued. Pilgrims still climb the steps and many who find they no longer need their crutches leave them behind as a testament to what they experienced.

This was what Corinne's dad needed. He needed a miracle.

Gregory was jaundiced. His skin and eyes had yellow tints. The cancer caused him to be tired most of the time. He also had back pain and severe stomach pain. The journey was difficult for him. When Corinne mentioned her concern he responded strangely.

"This is not a journey." Gregory wiped a tear from his eye. "It's a trip."

"All right," his daughter said, "then it's a trip. But whatever we call it, the drive here was hard on you and this climb is worse."

"I'm managing." Gregory smiled again and Corinne wondered if the tears might be from something other than fear or pain.

When Corinne was five years old her mom died in an accident. Corinne had been living with guilt for the last thirty years. She believed her mother's death was her fault.

Now her father had pancreatic cancer, which she also believed was her fault. The doctors gave him less than a year. When Gregory told Corinne, she knew she couldn't accept it. *I'm thirty-five, but I'm still not ready to lose Dad—to be an orphan. I may have killed my mom, but I will save my dad.*

"I know it will work," she said as she held his hand, "but it will be hard."

Gregory tilted his head and frowned. "Let's do this together, you and me."

Corinne looked straight at him, took in a breath and released it. "All right. We're on this trip together."

Gregory's grin was wide as they moved to the next step. A few steps later he was grimacing and holding his stomach.

"Are you okay?" Corinne asked, feeling her own stomach tighten.

"I'll be fine."

"We can rest a while longer if you'd like."

"That might be a good idea."

She prayed climbing these steps in search of a cure would be successful, a miracle from God brought about through their faith and determination, but as they sat there catching their breath she thought of Sisyphus rolling a boulder up a hill only to have it roll back again.

"Is this the hardest thing you've ever done?" she asked as they both turned to sit.

"No, not by a long shot." Gregory's head was tilted down as if he was looking toward the bottom of the mountain, but his eyes were glazed. "The hardest thing I ever did was getting out of bed the day after your mom died."

"Oh, Dad. I'm so sorry for what I did."

Gregory paused. "You were not responsible for your mom's death. You were a child and you acted like one." He reached over and took her hand. "She didn't lose her life because of you. You *were* her life."

Gregory Hedden
Woodstock

It was 1969. We were at the *Woodstock Music and Art Fair.*

My friends and I were sitting in the massive crowd about two-thirds of the way back from the stage, listening to John Sebastian. I loved his music, but I hadn't slept much the night before and I was exhausted. I closed my eyes and leaned back, wiggling my way through the people sitting behind me, so I could lie down while I listened to the songs. I fell asleep for a brief moment until I was woken by a foot on my belly. I grabbed the ankle that had disturbed me and started to twist it, but when I opened my eyes I found myself staring up a green skirt at two beautiful, fair-skinned legs leading to a pair of white panties stretched tightly over a woman's bottom. My jaw dropped and my eyes went wide.

"I'm sorry," the woman said. "Did I hurt you?"

I was too awestruck to answer.

"You were lower than everybody else. I thought this was an empty space. I was trying to make my way through the crowd."

"I'm okay," I told her.

"Then can you let go of my foot?"

I apologized and released her.

"Let me make it up to you," she said. "I'll take you on a trip."

I wanted to say "No harm" but this woman fascinated me. Instead I asked, "What do you mean?"

"Follow me and I'll show you."

I stood and got a better look at her. She had red hair, not carrot color like some redheads, but a strawberry blonde, way more toward the red side than the blonde. Her hair was parted in the middle and was long enough to fall over her shoulders and down another five or six inches.

She wore a loose green dress. It had long, full sleeves and a maxi skirt. She made it look perfect. She held the hem up above her knees. As I stared she let it fall. Her skin was pale, which was probably why she wore clothing that covered so much. The sun was intense and I was certain her skin could burn easily. She had no earrings, no necklace, no bracelets, and no makeup. She was very different from the other women at the festival.

I stood, glanced around and rubbed my forehead. The redhead picked up a large floppy hat which must have fallen off when I grabbed her. It was white with enough brim to keep her face in shade. She headed toward the back of the crowd where there was a guy in a black cape who was leading a sheep on a leash and carrying a sign that said something about not eating our animal friends.

"I'm leaving," I told Tim and Bobby, as I glanced around for a landmark. I located a large white stepvan behind the crowd. We were along a direct line between the stage and that truck. But I didn't intend to come back, so I said, "See you at the car later." We were parked about three miles away. We'd had to walk to the concert site, although after a few minutes we had hopped on the bumper of one of the slow-moving cars to lessen our walk.

"Hope you get lucky," one of them shouted. John Sebastian had just started singing *You Didn't Have to Be So Nice*. They were both swaying to the music.

"Sebastian wasn't supposed to be playing today, was he?" Tim asked.

Bobby mumbled a reply. I couldn't hear what he said.

I stepped around both of them and followed the woman. She looked back at me, waiting for me to catch up. When I reached her I said, "Now there's a character." I nodded at the sheep man.

"Maybe so," she agreed, "but I like his sign."

"You like animals?"

She tilted her head and smiled. "I don't eat them, if that's what you mean." She started to walk, holding her back straight, like a dancer.

"Then you're a vegetarian?" It was a stupid question, but I was trying to think of ways to keep the conversation going.

"It's a new thing for me. My mom said I could give up meat after I graduated, if I fixed my own dinners. So I've been cooking for myself for a couple of months now. Next year it will be harder. I'll be in college and on a meal plan."

"Oh?" I said, feeling my eyebrows raise. "Any chance you're going to Douglas? I just finished my freshman year at Rutgers."

"I never heard of Douglas, but next year I'll be at the University of North Carolina in Greensboro. That's where I'm from—Greensboro—but I'll be living on campus."

Wow. She came all the way from North Carolina, but all I said was, "From the south, huh? You don't sound like a southerner."

"I can sound like I'm from most anywhere. I want to be an actress, so I've worked hard at it. You want to hear New York?"

"I'm from Jersey. Can you do that?"

She nodded. "I wonduh if de sheep man has a dawg?"

We both laughed and I moved closer to her.

"So what's your name?" I asked, looking down at the ground. "I'm Gregory."

"I'm Cyn. It's short for Cynthia, but please call me Cyn."

"All right." I bit my lip and added, "I do have one more question. What is this trip you spoke of?"

The floppy hat Cyn wore and her full-length dress made her seem less trendy than the other women at the festival. The others had on tasseled crop tops with bell-bottom pants or peasant blouses with jeans or anything else that seemed like groupie fashion. They also wore things like suede bracelets, beaded necklaces, and colorful headbands. It was warm and they were dressed for comfort as well as fashion, but the dress Cyn wore must have felt like a sauna.

Cyn and I were outpacing everyone around us. She walked with the confidence of someone who believed in herself, as if she was one of the celebrities flown in by helicopter.

"Have you ever tried acid?" she asked.

I hated to seem inexperienced, but more than that I didn't want to lie. "No." I cleared my throat. "So that's the trip you spoke of?"

She nudged me with her shoulder. "I thought you seemed a bit naive."

I felt my stomach tighten.

"It's all right. Truth is I've never done acid either, but I came here with three other girls and one of them brought a stash. She told me I can have one. I want to try it, but not alone. I think I should take half and let you take the other half. We can go down this road together. What do *you* think?"

I'd smoked pot a few times, but LSD was another world. I'd heard all the stories about people dropping acid then thinking they could fly and jumping off the top of buildings. Of course, the only tall structures around here were the sound towers. The crews were keeping people off those. I could hear Santana playing. I didn't know what they were playing, but I recognized their sound.

"How much farther?" I asked Cyn, sounding like a kid on a family vacation.

"We're almost there." She nodded straight ahead.

"Oh." I looked around. I'd thought we were heading toward her car, but she was taking me to a row of port-a-sans. No wonder we'd been walking so fast. "Not a bad idea," I told her, chuckling.

She smiled. "You'll have plenty of time to think about my offer while we wait in one of those lines."

It was there, while we waited for the opportunity to shit, that our conversation began to get really weird.

Cyn narrowed her eyes. "What if the real world is the one people see when they're high? What if there's some chemical in our brains blocking us from seeing or feeling things and only when we swallow a dose of Sunshine can we know the truth? Do you really want to go through life without discovering what's out there? Do you want to be like the people in Plato's cave, seeing nothing but shadows on the wall and thinking that's all there is?"

I shrugged and looked in front of us. "I don't. But what if the only way we can stop that chemical from blocking the truth is by inhaling the stench from those toilets." I nodded at the port-a-sans. "Does that mean we should stick our noses down the hole?"

Cyn smiled, looked down, then rolled her eyes up at me. "That's ridiculous, but I can already smell the stink, so I'm doing what you suggested." She pinched her lips together. "You realize I was being serious, don't you?" I didn't answer. "There's so much more to life than what we see, for example, where were we before we were born and where will we be after we die?"

"You think dropping acid is the way to learn that?"

"Maybe. The only way to know for sure is to try. Now why don't you agree to take that trip with me?"

I let out a breath I didn't know I was holding. "Just a half, right?"

She nodded.

"Okay."

After we both used a port-a-san, we went on to

Cyn's campsite where I met her friend, Ellen, the one who had the acid. Ellen was wearing black jeans and a black tank top. She also had on three beaded necklaces and a thick brown belt that matched the color of her copper armband. The armband was decorated with swirling imprints that looked like waves. Her hair was long and beautiful, but the light brown color was not as striking as Cyn's.

The four young women had brought food in a cooler. Cyn offered me a peanut butter and jelly sandwich. Given that the lines were enormous for the rice and granola the organizers were handing out and I had brought only snacks such as pretzels, peanuts, chips, and cans of soda, this was a fairly good dinner. We ate together and talked about the trip we were planning.

"Two drug virgins," Ellen said, laughing. "This will be fun."

"We've both smoked pot," I told her.

She leaned over and pinched my arm, grinning. "That's like first base, honey."

"Yeah," Cyn said. "We're not ready to go all the way yet, so I thought we'd each take a half tablet."

I felt myself blush when she said "…all the way yet." I don't think either of the women noticed.

"I don't have tablets," Ellen told us. "What I've got is called Looney Tunes. It's acid on blotting paper. What I can do is put a dose in a glass of water and let it dissolve. You can each drink half. If you get the paper in your mouth, just spit it out." She paused. "Or I suppose you could chew it a little, to be sure you don't waste anything good."

She knew what she was doing, which seemed like a good thing. "Are you going to stick with us after we take it?" I asked.

"Of course. I'll be tripping too." I must have gone bug-eyed when she said that, because she added, "Don't worry. I'm used to this stuff. I won't let you do anything dumb."

When we were done eating we drank the magic water. As planned, Ellen drank a full glass while Cyn and I shared one. Ellen chewed the paper that had ended up in her mouth and spit it on the ground. Cyn ended up with the paper from *our* glass. When she was done chewing, she spat it into her hand and took it to a garbage bag they had hanging on the bumper of their car. She was about to throw it out when Ellen stopped her. "You don't want to be carrying that back to North Carolina with the rest of the garbage. If we get stopped, it will be every bit as incriminating as an unused dose."

Cyn tossed it into the bushes.

"What now?" I asked.

"We head back to the festival," Ellen said to both of us. "By the time we get there you should be flying."

She was right. We still hadn't reached the concert area when I started feeling it. There were no clouds that turned into eagles, terrifying dinosaurs coming at us from the woods or any of the other hallucinations I thought I might experience. Instead, everything became sharp and clear and so much more beautiful than before. It was like the difference between a Christmas tree that isn't decorated and one that's loaded with tinsel, lights, and shiny ornaments.

The first change I noticed was Cyn's lily-white face. She was bewitching with her hazel eyes and, of course, her red hair. It surrounded her face like a fireworks finale where the center of the display is encircled by explosions. When she spoke her mouth seemed so deep I felt as if I could crawl inside her, head first.

Cyn and I walked hand-in-hand, but she released her grip to touch my cheek, without missing a step. I loved the feel of her fingers on my skin. It sent shivers up and down my body as if I'd been touched by God.

Meanwhile, Ellen came up on the other side of me and put her arm around my shoulder. The three of us walked together with me in the middle of the two most magical women I'd ever known. Ellen had also begun to sparkle, although her brown hair didn't catch my eye the way Cyn's red did. She seemed to float as she walked, the way Jesus must have looked when he stepped onto the surface of the Sea of Galilee.

Cyn was right about LSD. With one-half dose in my body, the world had suddenly become clear and real. This was the greatest experience I'd ever had.

By the time Ellen, Cyn, and I reached the festival area, the LSD had kicked in and everything around us seemed to glow. We walked on, studying the crowds as we passed. I'm guessing it was around seven by this time. Music I couldn't recognize was playing. Donovan singing lead with The Grateful Dead backing him up? It didn't matter. I was digging it. I felt the notes run through my body. The acid not only made light intense, it made sound enormous and passionate.

We passed the area where plates of food were given out. As before, there was a huge line. I noticed one woman, who seemed older than me, waiting for her supper. Her hair was long and straight, kept in place with a green, narrow headband. She had two long braids, one on each side. Those braids were moving about like snakes. They had heads and fangs.

Except for her headband, the woman was naked and I was surprised by how clean she was. Maybe she'd just come from one of the streams where people were washing themselves. She was carrying a water jug and had a blue towel draped over her right arm.

There was one exception to her cleanliness. She had a gray mark on her elbow, as if she'd brushed up against a freshly painted fence. The drug in my system made me focus on that mark. I wanted to mention it to her, but I worried the words might not come out right, another side effect of the drug. I left it to the women handing out the food to say something. They seemed like nice people. They both had black hair. One had hers pulled back. The other had hers in pigtails. My mind was so confused I imagined they were twins, but the one with pigtails seemed to be fifty pounds heavier and the thin one could have been Asian. I was certain they would mention the mark on her elbow.

I thought everyone around me saw the mark with the same intensity I felt, but they didn't take the drug I'd taken. They couldn't see what I saw and they would never remember it, while every image I saw that day, real or unreal, burned into my memory.

I turned my attention from the naked woman. In front of her was a young man who might have been her boyfriend. He wore white slacks, as clean as every part of the woman other than her left elbow. He had on a polo shirt, white with blue stripes. Some of the stripes were made of triangles pointing up. Others were made of triangles pointing down. As I stared at the shirt those stripes seemed to vibrate with the sound of the music around us. I thought I saw them come to life. Were they reacting to the snakes on the head of his naked girlfriend? I didn't know. I turned to look at Cyn. She was staring at the same man I was staring at, but she seemed to be looking lower, at his white pants, just below his belt. I wondered if the drug was affecting her focus the way it was affecting mine.

Ellen's attention, however, was on the naked woman. She approached her and started to talk. I leaned forward.

"We want to go swimming," Ellen told her. "Do you know where the pond is?"

The woman shook her head, but the snakes pointed to the left.

"Is that the way?" I asked, nodding in the direction

her snakes had indicated.

The young man with the living shirt spoke up. "Yes. The pond is that way and there is a wonderful creek on the stage side with tiny rapids you can sit in."

When we walked on, I noticed the woman in the food line was not the only one who had stripped bare. Interspersed in the crowd were other men and women who had abandoned their clothing. Some danced, while others just ran around. The sheep man was naked now, carrying his animal rather than leading it on a leash. I wondered what it was about this place that made so many people want to shed their clothes.

On the way to the pond we passed a structure made of tree limbs lashed together. People were climbing it and jumping off, landing in a haystack. There was a man sitting on a flat platform lashed into the middle of that structure. He was playing his guitar, but the music from the stage was too loud for me to hear how good he was.

We passed the art display that was such a minor part of the festival, a hula hoop dome, a woman asleep on a pile of hay bales, a couple of young men milking a cow, a woman climbing to look at a cage filled with baby chickens, and a young mother in a lovely green and yellow dress with a very short skirt. She had pulled down one of her shoulder straps and was breastfeeding her naked child.

Finally, we reached the stream the man with the psychedelic shirt told us about. We discovered lots of people there who were bathing in their underwear. One woman was shaving her legs. That's the first time I saw a woman shaving her legs. I got down on one knee and stared at her razor. She seemed to wield it with so much skill, like a fencing master. The woman stood and moved away from me. I think she was upset. Ellen put her hand on my shoulder and told me I had to be careful. "You're not used to this," she said. I wasn't sure if she meant the acid or being around women who were shaving their legs.

I stood and stared at a different beautiful sight, a man and a woman with water from the rapids flowing around them. The woman's face tilted toward the sky as she leaned back against his shoulder. They didn't seem to mind me watching them.

We moved on to the pond where we found lots of naked swimmers. We saw an old pier with half the boards missing. It was sticking out into the water and lots of swimmers had gathered around it. One man sat on top while the others stood nearby. The water seemed shallow, but not too shallow to swim.

"Well here we are," Ellen announced. "I'm going swimming. Will you two join me?"

"I can't," Cyn told her. "The sun would be too much for my skin."

The sun wasn't as strong as it had been earlier, but I believed her anyway. I said I would stay with Cyn.

"Then you can watch my clothes," Ellen told me. She took everything off, including her armband, made a pile next to where Cyn and I sat and headed to the water.

There was less sparkle to the splashing in the pond than I had expected. Canned Heat had begun to play, which was nice. I recognized *Going up the Country* and started to sing along, although I didn't remember most of the words.

Cyn and I sat there watching the people enjoying the water. I took her hand and we leaned against each other. I was tired now and we still had a long walk back.

Ellen swam out to the center of the pond and back again, then walked up on shore. "It's time to head back," she said. "Would you bring my clothes?" I agreed as she sat next to me and put her sneakers on. They were Converse All Stars. I thought that was cool.

We passed the things on the way back we'd seen on the walk over. Everything looked a little different because it was twilight now. We walked the way we had walked before, with our arms around each other. I felt special, with

Cyn on my right and Ellen on my left.

Along the way, I heard my name called. Tim and Bobby had seen me and ran to catch up. We were walking in the path behind the crowd watching the concert, but it was still amazing they'd found me. I suppose having Ellen beside me helped. Both those guys had a second sense about naked girls.

"Where are you headed?" Bobby asked.

"To our campsite," Ellen told them. "You want to come along?"

"Sure," they said in unison.

After they joined us Cyn and I walked together, while Ellen walked between Tim and Bobby. We stopped where they were giving the food out because the line was shorter now. We waited for no more than ten minutes.

"This is so amazing," I told everyone who would listen. "When we passed by here earlier there was a naked lady in the line and now we've brought our own naked lady." I nodded at Ellen, who put on the widest grin I'd ever seen and bowed. "Only thing we're missing is a guy with bright white pants and a twirling shirt." Tim, Bobby, and I were all wearing T-shirts. Mine was plain blue, Bobby's was plain red and Tim's was black with a DC5 logo on the front and a concert date listed underneath. I think it said 1964, but that part was well worn.

Cyn held me tighter. "Maybe your shirt is ordinary, but you are special."

When we got back to Cyn and Ellen's campsite, the other two women were there: Linda and Patricia. We'd brought them each a plate of food, so we all ate together. After that, Cyn and I sneaked off to be alone. We found a soft grassy spot where we could lie down. The sun had set by now, so Cyn took off her clothes and I did the same. We stood facing each other. She lightly touched my body and I touched hers. The limited light from the crescent moon took some of the sparkle from her pale skin, but she still glowed. I felt the softness of her flesh and moved my hand between her breasts where I could feel her heart beating out the lyrics of *A Maid of Constant Sorrow*. Her body's song filled my head and as I slid my hand to its rhythm I touched every part of her and she did the same with me. She moved closer. We hugged. I pulled in a breath of her hair and lay down with her. Now, she hugged me with both her legs and her arms. I was on top of her, but holding myself up, so I could stare at her face as we made love. When we were done we rolled over, she rested her head on my chest and we fell asleep.

When I woke, Cyn and the other women were gone. Tim and Bobby sat beside me, waiting. They were smiling. I assumed they both got lucky, but I got so much more. I fell in love.

"She said to say goodbye," Tim told me, "and to tell you she had a wonderful time."

"I suggested we wake you," Bobby added, "but she said it was better this way."

I felt lonely as we walked back to Tim's car, passing close enough to the festival to hear Jefferson Airplane. We didn't stay to play in the mud, but some of it came home with us.

Gregory Hedden
UNC Greensboro

I should have been thrilled that I had been to Woodstock, what with all the publicity the festival received. We were treated like celebrities by anyone who didn't go. Still, all I could think of was Cyn. I had meant to get her last name and a phone number, an address, or any other way to reach her, but I hadn't. I put off asking her for too long. When she left suddenly I didn't get the chance. All I knew was her first name was Cynthia, she was from Greensboro, North Carolina and she was going to be a freshman at UNC Greensboro.

The remaining few weeks of summer were depressing. When I went off to Rutgers for my second year I was not excited. I chose my friend Bobby to be my roommate instead of having one assigned. We got along even though he called us the odd couple, after the Neil Simon play. I was a physics major and he was leaning toward theater.

Bobby's interest in acting reminded me of Cyn's comment that she wanted to be an actress. He was involved with a coffeehouse theater in downtown New Brunswick. I had him ask the man who directed most of the plays if he knew anything about the theater program at UNCG. It turned out he knew a professor there. Both men had been in some off-Broadway productions together before the professor accepted a teaching position down south.

This was good luck, but it didn't work out the way I'd hoped.

"He said he won't give you the man's name," Bobby told me.

"Why not?"

"He thinks you looking for some girl you met at Woodstock sounds creepy, especially since she didn't give you her number. He called it stalking and wants no part of it."

I couldn't think of anything to say. I just stood there with my mouth open, staring at my roommate.

"To be honest he has a point, but I sympathize with you. I think you should go down there."

"If I run around the UNCG campus asking people to help me find a redhead named Cynthia, your friend won't be the only person who thinks I'm a creep. And if I just wander around without speaking up, finding her will be almost impossible, right?"

"Not really," Bobby said, speaking in a steady voice. "If she wants to be a theater major, she'll be involved in plays."

"It's her freshman year. She'll be taking mostly general courses and probably have little time for anything else."

"She'll find time if she's serious about acting." Bobby sat up straight, still looking in my eyes. "Hang out by the theaters. Find a place to sit and read. Bring your textbooks, so you can keep up with the classes you'll miss while you're down there. You'll look like one of the local students, studying on the green. Then keep your eyes open for her. With that hair you described, she should be easy to pick out."

"I don't know," I muttered, speaking more to myself than to Bobby.

"Got any better ideas?"

I shrugged my shoulders.

"One more thing," Bobby said. "Wait to go until after the fall shows have their auditions, then look for the cast lists. They should be posted on a bulletin board in the department. Go through the major productions, of course, but also the student ones. See if anyone named Cynthia is listed and when you get a match, buy a ticket."

I laughed. "If the acting thing doesn't work out for you, you'd make a great detective."

***

I kept an eye on the auditions for the Rutgers and Douglas theater productions, figuring UNCG should be on a similar schedule. When the cast list for the fall production was posted at my school, I headed down to Cyn's hometown. It was a ten-hour drive from New Brunswick to Greensboro counting stops for meals. I rented a room in the Hotel King Cotton and spent my days studying my Rutgers' books on the Greensboro campus.

Searching for Cyn was more difficult than I had expected because theater classes were held in multiple buildings. I rotated from one spot to another, but after five days there was still no sign of her.

I checked the theater bulletin board. *The Roar of the Greasepaint – The Smell of the Crowd* was the fall production, but I didn't find any Cynthias in the cast. There were posters for a number of student projects, but the actors weren't listed for those.

There was one student show called *The White Lady*. I thought of Cyn's pale skin and decided a director looking for someone to play the title role would likely cast Cyn. I went to the theater box office to get a ticket where I discovered there was no cost.

"You still need a ticket," the woman in the booth told me. "It's a small theater."

"How small?"

"It's set up in a classroom. There are thirty chairs. Most of the seats will go to friends of the dancers in the class."

"Dancers?" I narrowed my eyes. "I thought this was a play."

"It's a dance. Dr. Fraser does one of these every year. I heard last year's was far-out."

She explained that the students in the class would be graded on their performances. Then she winked, leaned forward and said, "Applaud a lot so their grades go up."

I laughed at that and told her I would.

The dance was scheduled for Wednesday, the day after I got my ticket. When I showed up, I found a crowd mingling in the hall outside the classroom. I moved to a wall I could lean against while looking over the students. Most everybody was dressed in jeans and sweatshirts or bulky sweaters. The day was cool with a drizzling rain, so many were carrying jackets. I felt overdressed in my khakis and button-collar shirt, but there was one young woman dressed up more than me. She wore a black mini dress with long sleeves. It had a ruffled collar and matching cuffs. The skirt was very short. It came down to about three inches below her butt—when she was standing still.

She must have felt my stare because she turned and stared back. "Hey," she called to me. "Is that you, Woodstock boy?"

I raised my eyes from her legs to her face and discovered this young lady was Cyn's friend. "Ellen?"

"Yep. It's me." She walked over.

She was wearing makeup and looking fancy with glossy pink lipstick, matching eyeshadow, and black eyeliner. Except for her bare legs and the way she wore her hair down and loose, she didn't look much like the girl I had met at the festival. I smiled at her. "I didn't know you went to this school."

"I don't," Ellen said, "but I'm still friends with Cyn. I came to see her dance."

"She's in this show?"

"Of course she is." Ellen reached out and touched my arm. "But why are you here if you didn't know that?"

"All I knew about Cyn was her first name and she planned to go to school here. I couldn't stop thinking about her, so I came down to search."

"That was a long shot." Ellen winked at me. "Cyn's the only freshman in the class, but her teacher loves the way she looks. He chose the white lady theme for the class project because of that pale skin of hers, then he cast her as the lead dancer." She grinned. "You may have some competition."

"Maybe so," I rolled my eyes, "but here I am and it looks like I found her. Are you with anyone?"

"No. Wanna sit together?" She let go of my arm, but grabbed my hand, kissed me on my cheek, and led me toward the door which had just opened. "What's your name again? I don't remember."

I answered as we took seats together in the second-row center. The seats were on ascending platforms, in three rows of ten each.

The dance couldn't start until the audience settled, so while we were waiting I found out what Ellen had been up to. She'd started college at Elon, a school near Greensboro. She got through a few weeks, then grew bored and left. She hadn't bothered to drop her courses so she would fail them all. She seemed quite proud of that act of rebellion.

She was currently working as a hostess at a local Italian restaurant and had her own apartment. I didn't understand how she could afford the rent on the salary of a hostess, especially since she also told me she didn't have a roommate.

"Life is good," she said. She grabbed my arm again, pulled me close, and whispered, "You want a hit of acid before the show starts?"

"No. I'm good." Her offer helped me understand how she paid her bills.

Someone switched off the classroom lights, leaving us in total darkness. The music started. I recognized the piece, although I couldn't name it. It started slow and soft. Ellen reached over, grabbed my thigh and squeezed.

Apparently, she wanted assurance I was still there. If she was tripping, as I was certain she was, she might have thought I had magically disappeared.

A spotlight came on, focused on a woman lying face down on the floor. Her hair was pulled up into the same broad-brimmed, white hat Cyn had worn at Woodstock. That's how I knew it was her. She was dressed in a two-piece, white leotard. The leotard's color blended into her pale skin.

She started to writhe about, rotating her head, rubbing her body against the floor. There was a sexuality to the way she squirmed about on her belly and chest.

Six other women came onto the stage wearing identical loose-fitting dresses that looked like plain white nightgowns. By this time the music was loud and wild. Four of the dancers got down in similar positions to Cyn's. One of the two still standing ran toward us and picked up her skirt, raising the hem to mid-thigh. The other standing woman began to move around the stage area, pulling her arms up like an eagle's wings, then touching them above her head, making fists and bringing them down over the front of her body.

Cyn stood and threw her hat toward the audience. It came straight for Ellen since we were sitting in the center. Ellen caught it.

My jaw dropped as I leaned forward. I had known this was Cyn since the lights went on, but this was the first time in months I had seen her face. Woodstock came rushing back to me, the way she felt in my arms, the sweet smell of her skin.

Her red hair fell over her shoulders. I could still remember the silky feel between my fingers and the scent more seductive than an earthy wine. She turned toward the audience as the other dancers formed a group behind her. They moved as one, each woman raising her arms and twisting at her waist, forming a scene like a field of wheat blowing in the wind. Cyn began to weave in and out among the other dancers. When she returned to the front of the group, she spun in one sharp motion, lifting her right leg so high it touched her head. I was amazed by that move.

The women were all lyrical and beautiful. Their arms moved gracefully, their shoulders dipped in unity and their hips gyrated like spiritual cyclones. The dancers seemed to fly across the stage with the grace of migrating birds and the never-ending rhythm of ocean waves. Cyn was at the center of this beauty and, when it was over, I was more in love than I had thought possible.

The lights went out. We sat in darkness until someone switched the classroom lights on. All the dancers were now in a line across the stage area. They bowed, then filed out of the classroom as we stood, applauded and shouted with joy. Before that performance, I had no idea how wonderful a dance concert could be.

Less than ten seconds after the cast filed out of the classroom they came back. They were out of character, greeting the friends who had come to see them and accepting compliments.

Ellen waved to Cyn as she walked toward us. I don't think Cyn recognized me until she was close. Perhaps her eyes were on Ellen, but when she saw me standing beside her friend, her eyebrows shot up and she smiled. When she reached us she hugged Ellen, leaving me standing there, feeling awkward.

"This is a surprise." Cyn turned to me. She stepped closer as if she was going to hug me next. When her face was near mine she said, "What are you doing here?" She wrinkled her nose slightly.

This was not the reaction I'd expected.

Ellen's eyes were shining. Cyn's were squinting.

I felt an ache growing in my chest. It stopped when Cyn reached out and hugged me longer than she had hugged Ellen, but I was still getting mixed signals.

"Come on, both of you," Cyn said. "I want you to meet Dr. Fraser."

"Fraser?" I asked.

Ellen laughed. "That's the professor who likes her skin."

Cyn rolled her eyes. "Give me a break, Ellen."

Ellen and I greeted Dr. Fraser and congratulated him on the dance. After what Ellen had told me about his interest in Cyn's appearance, I was concerned she might be in a relationship with him. But when I met her teacher, he treated Cyn like he treated all the dancers gathered around him. *Nothing special there.*

Ellen suggested we go out for something to eat. I was pleased with that and I think Cyn was as well. She was looking straight in my eyes and smiling. She took back her hat and headed to the dressing room, while Ellen and I went to our seats and waited for her to change.

I looked at Ellen and said, "Tell me more about what you've been up to."

She poked me in my side. "You don't want to know about me. Why don't you ask about Cyn?"

"All right, what's she been up to?"

"We were best friends when we were kids and we stayed close during high school. I don't want to give up on our relationship, but Cyn and I are very different." Ellen crossed her legs and straightened her tiny skirt as best she could. "She is a talented woman. I am, let's say..." She looked toward the front of the classroom before adding, "...less so. Her goal is to become an actress. My goal is to have the best time possible while I'm alive. She thinks of the future in terms of where she wants to be years from now. I think of the future in terms of what I'm going to do tonight. We can still have a meal together and talk, but, unless one of us changes, we'll never be as close as we were when we were little. Our mindsets are worlds apart."

"If she wants to be a professional actress, what is

she doing here?"

"She can prove herself while going for a degree she can fall back on. At least, that's what she told me."

"Then she doesn't want to go to New York or California?"

"No. Well, not yet anyway."

I felt my shoulders droop and Ellen noticed. "That disappoints you?"

"A little. New York would be close to me."

She shook her head and smiled. "Don't get ahead of yourself, Gregory. You'll scare her off."

Cyn came back into the classroom wearing a red turtleneck sweater with blue jeans, sneakers, and no hat.

"Can we go to Ham's?" she asked.

I turned to Ellen and raised my eyebrows.

"It's a college hangout. It'll be crowded and we may even run into some of the other dancers there. It will probably take us a while to get a table, but once we're seated they won't push us out."

"So you're good?" Cyn asked her.

"Sure and I can drive."

We could have walked. The light rain had stopped but the evening air was brisk.

The place had huge windows looking out on the small parking area. Across from the windows there were poster-size photos of antique cars. It was casual with plenty of square tables in the smoke-filled dining area. Some of the tables had been moved together for groups larger than four people. Ellen seemed to enjoy standing out in her little black dress. Heads turned when we entered the restaurant. We got a booth right away. I sat on one side. Ellen and Cyn sat on the other.

I wanted a beer but North Carolina law didn't allow it. Instead, we each had a coke and I ordered a dish of fries with gravy to share. We started bantering until we grew tired of the small talk. That's when I asked Cyn, "Why didn't you wake me that morning, when you left Woodstock?" My voice dropped as I added, "I wanted to say goodbye."

Even in the dim restaurant light, I could see Cyn's face turn red. She leaned across the table and said, "I didn't want you to see me cry."

I stared at her lips. "Over me?"

"Yes, but not only you." She put her hands in her lap. She rocked back and forth ever so slightly. "My time at Woodstock was exciting and amazing, but it was also comforting."

I tilted my head.

She seemed to notice my confusion. "I wanted to spend the rest of my life at the festival, even though I knew it would end and everyone would go home. As for us, we had to leave early Sunday morning because we had a long drive, especially since we knew it would take a lot of time just to get out of the festival area."

I understood what she meant. It had been difficult for me to adjust to those three days ending.

Cyn bit her cheek. "You would be surprised how often I think of the weird way we met, me stepping on your stomach and you grabbing my foot. I also think about walking with you and watching the swimmers."

"Including me, right?" Ellen said, laughing.

"Of course," Cyn told her, then, turning back to me, she said, "I miss all those adventures."

"Do you think it was the drugs?" Maybe I shouldn't have brought it up, but the great time I had that day was partly due to the acid Ellen gave us.

Cyn shook her head. "I did think it was the LSD, so I tried it again. The second time was different. I kept picturing a big guy in a wife-beater shirt. He was furious with me. He wrestled me to the ground and punched me violently. I was so scared I wet my pants. I mean it. I actually did. But the guy wasn't there. I was alone with

Ellen, who was trying to hold my hand and help me through my fears. I'm never taking acid again. That's for sure."

"It was just one bad trip," Ellen told her. "You'll be missing out on a lot."

Cyn reached over and took my hand. "I needed you with me. It wasn't the festival that comforted me. It was you."

I could feel my pulse in my throat. I couldn't speak and the girls didn't either until Ellen finally asked about my life since Woodstock. I took a deep breath and explained I was still at Rutgers, still considering a major in physics as I had told Cyn back in August. "Although, I'm not sure if physics is my goal or one my parents have pushed on me."

"You didn't drop out?" Ellen asked, probably thinking of her own situation.

"No. I took a week off to come here. I'll be missing some classes, but I'm keeping up with the textbooks as best I can. I think I'll be alright if I get back on time."

Ellen leaned in toward me. "So when are you leaving?"

"Tomorrow morning."

"And where are you staying?"

"I've got a room at the Hotel King Cotton. It's about a half-hour walk from here." I looked at Ellen as I answered, but my gaze turned back to Cyn.

Cyn smiled. "I always wondered about that place. It's supposed to be nice—classic."

"It is. The rooms aren't so special, but the lobby is unreal. The ceiling is two stories up, with huge chandeliers. There's wicker furniture. It looks very southern, at least it does to a Yankee like me."

Ellen laughed. "Why don't you two go there? I've got something else I need to do." Her excuse for leaving was lame, but I appreciated it.

Cyn's eyes sparkled. "Sure. When will I have

another chance like this?"

***

Cyn was more impressed with my room than I imagined she would be. It was large, compared with motel rooms. There were two double beds, a writing table, and a TV on a sideboard across from a couch. Most everything in the room was brown, from the bureaus to the bedspread, although the couch was red leather.

We turned on the TV, flipped through the channels and found one where Hitchcock's *The Birds* was playing. It had just started, so we stuck with that.

"You want a drink?" I asked Cyn around the time Rod Taylor mistook Tippi Hedren for a shopgirl and asked about lovebirds. "I have a fifth of Dewer's with me." She shrugged so I told her, "That's bourbon."

She rolled her eyes. "I know what it is."

I felt foolish for assuming she didn't, but when she signaled she wanted the drink by nodding toward the bottle I poured us each a glass. I mixed in a little more water than whiskey, figuring neither Cyn nor I wanted more than we could handle. Yet I did need something to ease my nerves. This was the first time since August I'd been alone with her. I didn't want to act like a fool.

I said, "Cheers," and we each took a large gulp.

We brought our drinks to the couch where we could watch the TV from a better angle, at least that was my excuse. We each had a couple more sips, then I set both our glasses on the floor, off to the side of the couch. I sat next to her and put my arm around her shoulder. She placed her hand on my leg and moved her fingers, massaging my thigh. I leaned closer to her as she put her head in the crook of my neck. Meanwhile, on the TV, Tippi Hendren was attacked by the first seagull.

This was the moment I'd been dreaming about since we were together at the festival. She was as excited to be alone with me as I was to be with her. I could tell as we leaned toward each other and kissed.

My body tingled when I tasted her mouth. She hadn't been wearing lipstick in August, so this time was different, not the way she tasted as much as the slick sensation, especially when she touched my tongue with hers. She was moist, smooth, and I was dizzy, from her more than the liquor. I could tell the difference.

I slid my lips along her face to the side of her neck where I breathed her in. She must have taken a quick shower in the dancers' dressing room because her skin had the green, flowery smell of fresh soap, while her red hair smelled of strength and passion.

I pressed her down, gently, until she was lying on the couch. I moved her sweater as I shifted my face to kiss her firm, dancer's stomach. I tickled her navel with my tongue then kissed all the skin around it. I savored the motion of her body, feeling the movement of her muscles. She breathed in and out, intense now, my head riding the soft flow of her body. I stopped my kisses when she moved to sit up then watched as she pulled off her top. Cyn was wearing a red bra, one that matched her sweater and drew attention to her hair. She quickly took it off as well and pulled me to where I could bury my face in her chest.

I moved back to stare at her, so I could etch her beauty in my memory, the white of her soft skin as pure as spring, highlighted with the red of her hair, the green in her hazel eyes, the rose of her lips, and the pink of her nipples.

Cyn stood and I followed. She took my hand. She led me toward the bed, but stopped before we got there so we could hug again and take off the rest of our clothes.

When we made love at Woodstock we'd been tripping on music and drugs and we were surrounded by thousands of rebellious young people who made the whole world feel magical. All that day I'd been fascinated by the way Cyn moved and talked. When we lay together in that patch of grass I was thrilled with her body. Cyn said she felt comforted by me, but she was the one who had put us both at ease. She was the leader. I followed and I fell in love.

This time Cyn and I were alone and when our bodies connected I could feel her soul and knew she could feel mine.

I couldn't let her go when we were done. I was on my back. She was on top of me. We were still panting, our breathing a synchronized duet. When she finally moved off me, there was joy for what we had experienced mixed with sadness because we had to separate. I stayed on my back as she twisted around so she could lay her head on my chest, but soon after that she moved again. She rolled to lie on her stomach, then raised herself on her elbows and looked in my eyes. She grinned. "I don't want to end this, but I have to get some sleep. I've got a morning class."

"You'll sleep here, won't you?"

"I was hoping you would ask." She laughed a little. "I'd love to."

"Can I take you to breakfast in the morning?"

"I'd love that, too, if we can get an early start and do fast food. There's a Hardee's near campus. My class is at nine."

We woke early, showered, dressed and left the hotel by seven-fifteen. We made it to Hardee's and finished breakfast by eight, so we had about a half-hour to kill. I bought us each a second cup of coffee, which we drank while we talked.

"I've never seen you act," I told her, "but I've seen you dance. I bet you're a fabulous actress." I reached across the table and touched her arm. "When did you decide this is what you wanted to do with your life?"

Cyn looked at the ceiling and back at me. "I took a speech class in high school. The teacher liked my style and suggested I audition for a one-act play he was directing for the community theater. It was *The Lesson* by Ionesco. I played the pupil."

"I don't know that one."

"I didn't think you would." Cyn put her palms together and touched her lips. "It was my first role and a rough one. My character was murdered on stage, in a very violent way, almost a rape. But I discovered how much I loved taking on a character's problems. Acting enables me to become someone else. It's like traveling, only instead of going to another place, I get to become another person— body, mind, and soul."

"It's not fame you're after?"

She grinned. "I wouldn't mind being famous, but there's more to it than that. After my first show closed, I understood my dream. I want to perform with the best and they are in New York. Someday I hope to find out if I can make it there."

My heart started to pound.

"Your dream shouldn't wait," I said as I reached across the table and played with the ends of her long hair. "You should go to New York."

Cyn leaned toward me. "How can I do that?"

"My roommate and I are moving off campus next semester. You could live with us." I winced. "I mean with *me*, of course. We'll have our own room."

She pulled away and stood. "I don't understand. You'll be in New Jersey, right?"

I looked into her eyes. "You can take a bus to New York every day—or a train." I held my head up and shoulders back. "You met my roommate, Bobby, at Woodstock. He wants to be an actor, too. He told me there's this outta sight place in Manhattan called The Green Room. You can stay there all day with other actors, making friends and connections. There's a bulletin board where they list opportunities and they also answer your phone, so you won't miss a call from one director while you're out auditioning for another."

She picked up the salt shaker and fidgeted with it. "You've thought this through, haven't you?"

"Is that bad?"

"I guess not." She set the salt down and stood. "It's just that—I need some time." She took a step toward the door.

It was still too early to be heading to her class, but I followed her anyway. "We'll be signing the lease around the first of January," I told her, "so we can have it for next semester. That should work for you. I imagine you'll want to finish your semester here, right?"

"I'll need to get a job, to have money for my part of the rent, for bus fare, for whatever The Green Room costs and for other things." Her voice trailed off.

"Don't worry about the rent. Bobby and I got that. Bobby says you might need to kick in a little for food, but we can work all that out. You could easily get a job in New York."

"You talked this over with your roommate?"

I nodded.

"Before you drove down here?"

I nodded again.

"But you didn't even know if you could find me."

"I hoped I would and I planned for the best."

Cyn frowned and looked down. "There's another thing about this plan of yours I need to know."

I stopped and waited for her to explain.

"What are we?' she asked, turning toward me.

"I don't understand."

"You and I have only been together a couple of times, up at Woodstock and here in Greensboro. Now you're asking me to move in with you? If I say yes, will that make me your girlfriend? Or am I just a roommate?"

"I know what I want you to be."

"Then tell me."

"I want us to be a couple. I've known that since the first time I saw you."

"The first time you saw me, you were looking up my skirt."

I felt my body grow tense. "That wasn't my fault and you know it." I was speaking too loudly. "You stepped on me."

"Are you angry?"

I shook my head, but her reaction to my offer *was* bumming me out.

"This brings us to another problem," she said. "Say I move in with you and we have a fight, a big one. What then? Do I have to move out? If so, where do I go?"

We stopped at a light to cross Market Street. "All right. Here's the deal. If you come to New Jersey and move in with me, I won't assume anything about our relationship, but I do want us to be together. We haven't known each other very long…"

"There's an understatement."

I spoke a little louder. "…but sometimes opportunities come along when you're not expecting them. If you don't jump when they're in front of you, they may never come again." I paused. "So what do you want?"

She pressed her lips together, then said, "Come with me to my Western Civ lecture. If you do that, I promise I'll think over your offer."

"This may be your only chance," I reminded her.

"That's true." She sighed. "But remember, if I do go to New Jersey, you won't have to work hard to get me to want to be with you. I'm already there."

Gregory Hedden
Together Again

The ride back to New Jersey seemed shorter, although I traveled the same highways I'd been on when I drove south. Perhaps this was because I was familiar with some of the landmarks but I believed it had more to do with the regret I felt as I headed away from Greensboro. On the way to Cyn, I longed to be there and each mile I drove seemed to take hours. On the way back, I didn't want to leave and each mile seemed to fly by too quickly.

When I pulled into the student parking lot at Rutgers it was after eleven. I carried my suitcases to my room and went straight for the hall phone. I hadn't left North Carolina until after Cyn and I had lunch together. I planned to leave earlier but it was too hard to say goodbye.

Cyn picked up after a single ring. She was also in a dorm with a hall phone, so she must have been waiting for my call. "Gregory?"

"It's me." I cleared my throat before saying, "I miss you already."

"I was worried," Cyn told me. "It's a long drive. I should have made you go earlier, so you wouldn't have been driving after dark."

"I was fine, not tired at all."

There was a pause, then she said, "I...uh...I miss you, too." I heard her sniffle.

"I'm going to take another week off, so I can go down there again."

"You can't. It's hard enough to make up for losing a week. You need to go to your classes. And what about your labs? You can't keep missing those."

I could feel my heart beating. "What difference

does it make? You're all I can think about."

"You have to concentrate—and do well enough to graduate. You were right when you told me I'm wasting my time in classrooms, but that isn't true for you."

"You're saying you're coming here?"

"Yes, I am." I heard her take a quick breath. "I want you to know something else. I feel empty when I'm not beside you." She paused again. "What I mean to say is I won't be heading to New Jersey just to chase my theater career. I want to be an actress and I want to be with you. I don't see any reason why I can't have it all."

My body tingled. "No reason at all, Cyn."

"I'll finish the semester like you suggested then I'll move up there. I promise I'll be with you in a few months. I love you."

"I love you, too," I whispered back.

***

I wrote a letter a day, starting in the morning, adding to it each time I returned to my room and mailing it in the evening. She did the same and I checked my box every afternoon. If there was no letter one day, the next day there would be two. We were both determined to make this relationship last.

We decided to speak on the phone once a week. Long-distance rates for out-of-state calls were too expensive to talk every day. When the time arrived to call her, I always went to a phone booth in the student center. There was more privacy in a booth than at the hall phone.

The next four calls felt much like the first, lots of mushy language and kissing the phone. The fifth, however, was different.

Cyn picked up the phone before it rang twice. She cleared her throat and told me, "I miss you." She always said that first thing, before even a "Hello."

I paused for a moment before saying, "I miss you,

too." There was something off about her voice. She didn't sound lonely, she sounded scared. There was another pause, so I said, "Are you having second thoughts about coming up this way?"

"No."

"Please let me know if you start to. I don't want to lose you. I'll drop out of school if I need to and move to Greensboro."

"Don't do that. Stick with our plan."

"I will as long as you do."

"You don't have to worry. I'll move there as soon as the semester is over."

"You promise?"

"Of course I do, if you still want me."

Cyn's letters showed no sign of anything wrong. When we were talking I continued to notice pauses in our conversation and slight changes in the tone of her voice but I put those out of my thoughts. I trusted her reassurances.

***

When the semester ended I moved out of the dorm and into the apartment I would be sharing with Bobby. It was two stories with a staircase near the front door. The place wasn't large but it would fit the three of us. Upstairs we had two bedrooms and a bathroom with a tub/shower. The bedrooms were on the front and back sides of the apartment. They were separated by the bathroom so Bobby wouldn't hear everything that went on in our room.

Two men sharing a bathroom with a woman would be difficult but we would adjust. Downstairs was a space that was two-thirds living room and one-third dining room. There was also a small kitchen next to that great room. We had a single phone in the living room section which didn't provide any privacy. When Bobby was home I planned to head back to the student center when I made my weekly calls. It was inconvenient but there would only be a few more before she'd be in New Jersey—living with me.

During our final phone call, one day before she was to move into our apartment, Cyn said, "There's something we need to discuss before I drive there."

I started to speak, but all that came out was a slight gasp.

"Can you hear me?" she asked.

"Y-y-yes," I stammered. I took a breath to recover my voice and asked, "Are you changing your mind?"

"No. Never. But what I have to say might change our plans."

"Change them how?

"That's what we need to talk about."

We were both quiet for a short time. I didn't know what to say and I didn't know why she wasn't speaking.

"I'm pregnant," she told me at last, in a voice so low I almost couldn't hear her.

"What?"

"Pregnant," she repeated a little louder. I tried to say something but nothing came out. When I didn't speak she asked, "Do you still want me there?"

"Of course I do." I leaned against the phone booth wall so I wouldn't fall over. "It's just that—you've kinda shocked me."

"You probably won't ask this, so I'll just come out and tell you. The baby's yours. I haven't been with anyone else since Woodstock and I wasn't pregnant before or after the festival. Our child was conceived in your hotel room in Greensboro."

"Why didn't you tell me when you first knew?"

"Because I didn't want to fight with you about options. I don't want an abortion and I don't want to give her up for adoption. I plan to raise this baby. You can be as much a part of our lives as you wish. That's up to you."

My entire body shook as I squeaked out, "Her?"

"Yes. That's what the ring gender test says."

"The ring what?"

"It's a centuries-old way of knowing if a baby is a boy or a girl. Ellen showed it to me. She tied a ring on a string and held it over my womb. It swung in a circle which means you're going to have two women living with you soon, if you want us."

***

When Cyn arrived we hugged and kissed and said how much we missed each other. I brought her suitcases in and told her she could unpack. I also warned her I didn't know how long we'd be living there. That was a surprise to her.

I shrugged. "Bobby was happy to have you living with us when you were a young actress looking for work in New York. When he learned you are now an expectant mother his tune changed. He doesn't like the idea of living with a newborn."

"I'm still an actress."

"Are you?" I frowned and asked, "Can we sit down for a few minutes and talk about our situation? Would you like a glass of wine?"

"No." She glanced down at her belly. Her doctor had suggested she give up alcohol until after the baby arrived.

I rubbed my chin and looked around. "How about a cup of coffee or tea?"

"It's too late for caffeine. Do you have any herbal tea?"

"Bobby has some chamomile."

We moved to the kitchen table. Cyn took a seat while I put a pot of water on the stove.

"Why isn't Bobby here?" she asked, glancing around the apartment.

"He's with a friend. I asked him to let us have one night alone."

"And he agreed?"

"Yes."

"That was nice of him."

"Here's the thing. My parents know about our situation. They were surprisingly understanding. My mom was actually excited about the news, although she warned me to be careful not to marry for the sake of the baby because that can cause problems."

"What did you say to that?"

"Not a thing." I took in a breath and let it out slowly. "I love you, Cyn, and want to spend the rest of my life with you. I'm certain I will love our child but you are the one I care about now. I wasn't going to argue about something that isn't an issue. Mom said she and my father want to be a part of our baby's life whatever happens. She told me they are willing to rent an apartment and pay for our groceries as long as I stay in school and keep my grades up."

Cyn sat up straight. "That's good, right?"

"It means we can be together without me dropping out. But keeping my grades up will take a lot of time. They insist I maintain a decent GPA, at least 4.0 on the 5.0 scale they use here."

"Still, we're okay, right?"

"We are. What I'm saying is I can't raise our child alone."

"I'm not asking you to do that!"

"You say you're still an actress. Does that mean you plan to audition in New York? What happens if you get cast in a show that keeps you out every night? What happens if you get cast in a touring company?"

"You're asking me to give up my dream?"

"A baby changes everything. I'm asking you to be flexible."

"Flexible? That's what you call it? Sounds as if I have to do *all* the changing. How does this arrangement affect *your* life? You're still going to classes. You'll be leading the life you led before I arrived!"

My mind was racing, searching for answers. "What do you want me to do? Drop out and get a job?"

She reached both her hands up into her thick, red hair and seemed to pull on it. "Would that be so bad?" she asked, raising her voice. "We could pay our own way. Our child could be in daycare during the day and home with you at night. When I'm not in a play I could take over."

This wasn't going right. She'd only been here for about an hour and already we were fighting. I could feel my jaw clench. Her eyes were growing cold. My heart was pounding.

I took a deep breath, let it out and changed the subject. "Tell me about your parents."

"What about them?" Her breathing slowed down somewhat. She was trying to avoid fighting with me, as I was with her.

"Did you tell them you're pregnant?"

She smiled. "They're Southern Baptists. They reacted how you would expect them to. They were angry. They said I was foolish for giving in to my urges. That's the word they used." We both laughed and I was feeling less tense. "Once I told them I had decided to keep the baby, they calmed down. I think they were expecting a fight, thinking I would refuse to carry her to term. When they learned I intended to raise my child they were pleased with me."

"*Our* child," I said.

"Of course."

"It should have been my decision as well as yours."

"Our child but *my* body. That's what makes the difference."

"I understand. But it isn't only your responsibility and now you want me to drop out of college."

Cyn crossed her arms as her eyes went wide. I'd spoken without thinking. The fight was starting up again. I couldn't change the subject a second time. I would try to appease her somehow, without giving in on my principles.

That didn't work. We stayed at each other's throats until after midnight when we couldn't put off going to bed any longer.

We moved to the bedroom. She stared at the bed. I could tell she was unwilling to admit she didn't want to sleep with me because I felt the same way. Changing out of my street clothes with the fight still swirling in my head was awkward. We got into our night clothes while facing away from each other, and then I turned to look.

As soon as I saw Cyn in her white, sleeveless nightgown all the anger slipped from me. I stepped up to her wearing my boxers and a T-shirt. She didn't move. I held her and kissed her, suddenly longing for the taste of her mouth. She pulled away at first, but I wouldn't let go and soon she was kissing me back. She whispered in my ear, "Make love to me, Gregory. Please. There's no reason to hold back." I did as I was told—three times.

Finally, we were free again, free of anger, worry, and doubt in each other. This was going to work. Cyn and I were going to be forever. Nothing else was important.

We woke up the next morning, put on a pot of coffee, sat down together and began discussing compromises. We were still wearing what we'd slept in, but Cyn put on my robe in case Bobby walked in on us.

She was shaking her head back and forth. "I'm going to have to put off professional acting, aren't I?"

I looked down at my coffee. "Professional, maybe." I moved my gaze back up and added, "But not all acting. There must be some good amateur theaters around here. We can ask Bobby when he gets back."

"That's a commitment, too. Between the rehearsals and performances there will be plenty of times when I can't be home with our girl. You'll have to step up."

"And I'll do that. Maybe my parents can help, too."

"What about my parents?"

That was a strange thing to ask. They didn't live close enough to help. "What about them?"

"I've been thinking of a plan that might work for both of us. We stay up here for this semester and this coming summer. That's long enough for me to have the baby while you're still working on your degree. Next year we move to Greensboro. I start up again at UNCG and you transfer to a school in that area. UNCG is an option, but there are others. I'm certain plenty of the Greensboro schools have physics majors."

I heard what she was saying and it did make sense, sort of. We'd both be giving in a little. That's what compromise was. Cyn kept talking, explaining the second part of her plan. "We move in with my parents. That way they'll be there to take care of the baby when we both need to be in school."

My jaw dropped. All I knew of them was they were Southern Baptists. I had some preconceived ideas about Southern Baptists.

"I guess I could go for that," I told her in a quiet voice. More than anything else I wanted to stay with her.

"There is one catch to this plan." Cyn sat up straight and folded her arms across her chest. "We'll need to get married. They want that and so do I."

I heard the apartment door open and close. The door was visible from the kitchen, so we both turned to see Bobby was back.

"Come on over," I told him.

He stepped our way, still wearing his winter coat. "It's been a while, Cyn. How have you been since Woodstock?"

"I've been well. I've heard we've got some things in common."

"I'm an actor, if that's what you mean."

"It is."

Bobby raised his eyebrows. "I'm enjoying school so

a career in New York is still a few years off." He paused. "Tell me about yourself. I thought you were brave to drop out the way you did. What are your plans now that you have…uh…one in the oven?"

"In the oven?" Cyn laughed again. "You don't have to tiptoe around it. I'm knocked up."

"I guess you are." Bobby laughed. "So what are your plans?"

"We were just talking about that. We're thinking marriage might be a good idea."

He gasped, turned to me and asked, "This is okay with you?"

I stood up. "What we decide is our own business."

He looked at me, then Cyn, then back at me. "I guess it is. Sorry."

Cyn frowned. "I think he's got a good question. Is this okay with you?"

I put my hand on her shoulder. "All that's important to me is staying with you."

Bobby didn't seem to hear or care about my answer. He addressed Cyn. "You have a baby and you will spend the next fifteen to twenty years raising him."

"Her," she corrected.

"All right. Her." He took in a breath. "You are a beautiful girl even when you're sitting down—wearing Gregory's robe. You also have a very unique appearance. It would still be a gamble for you to go to New York, but the odds are in your favor, if you have any talent at all."

"She does," I said too loudly. "She is great."

Bobby continued speaking to Cyn. "If you wait 'til you age out, you might not be able to make a name for yourself."

I could feel my body growing tense as he kept talking. "Go easy on her, man."

Cyn held her hand up for both of us to stop. "I know everything you're saying, Bobby. I don't need a man to tell me this. It's my choice to make and I've made it."

***

We hadn't found a place of our own, so we were going to be living with Bobby until that happened. Fortunately, an apartment identical to Bobby's opened up in his complex a couple of weeks later. We grabbed it, signing the contract the next day. It took us a week or so to move our stuff and buy some additional furniture.

Soon, Cyn and Bobby were getting along like brother and sister. Bobby picked out a couple of shows in New York for the three of us to see. We also went out to dinner as a threesome more often than we did as a couple.

At one point, Cyn suggested we fix Bobby up with Ellen. "He might have been with her at Woodstock, you know."

"Might have?"

"Patricia and Linda kept talking about Tim most of the way home, so I think Ellen and Bobby probably wandered off after we did. Didn't the guys talk on your drive home?"

I shook my head. "They did but mostly about the music and the crazy people we saw up there. The only thing Bobby mentioned about Ellen was how she walked naked through the crowds." I smiled at Cyn. "He was impressed with that. He called it street theater and said it was brave." When Cyn didn't react I added, "If he said anything more personal I didn't hear it. I had my mind on you."

"Brave?" Cyn asked. "That's the word he used?"

"Uh...yes."

"That's something, isn't it?"

"They've got separate lives in separate places. I don't see any way it would work out." What I did not mention was my concern about drugs because Ellen was still Cyn's best friend. Bobby wasn't big on recreational use and I didn't see how he could date Ellen and stay clean.

The subject was dropped but not forgotten.

***

The problem with having Bobby as a good friend was that Cyn was constantly reminded about New York theater. He was always talking about the latest shows, not only Broadway but off-Broadway and the experimental theaters scattered around the city. When she heard his comments, she would hunch her shoulders while holding her arms across her belly. I could tell she was thinking about missed opportunities.

I was thrilled with the idea of marriage and agreed to move to North Carolina after the next semester. Even applying to another school went well. UNCG had a physics major, so I tried there. I was accepted and pleased to discover all my credits were transferable. I would be going to the same school as Cyn. Yet she still didn't seem happy and I didn't know how to cheer her up.

There were also the normal problems of pregnancy. She had passed the time of morning sickness before arriving in New Jersey so I wasn't coming back to the apartment to find her leaning over the toilet. But there were other issues. Her belly seemed to grow every day. So did her breasts, which became quite sensitive. She had some minor acne and some darkening of the skin around her navel and on the inside of her thighs. She was upset by the changes to her skin. I tried to tell her she was still beautiful. If she listened she didn't believe me.

I wasn't lying to her. Even with those few pregnancy blemishes, Cyn was the most beautiful woman I'd ever known. That fact made me wonder whose genes our child would inherit. Cyn was a couple of inches shorter than my five foot nine. Our heights matched well. Perhaps our daughter would be similar. I had love handles while Cyn's pre-pregnancy waist had been as trim as a porcelain figurine. I didn't care if she lost that extra weight but I hoped our daughter wouldn't inherit her waistline from me. My dark hair was starting to thin yet I still had my widow's peak. I also had dark eyes and skin that stayed tan without time in the sun, which was good since living with Cyn meant staying in the shade. Overall, I hoped our daughter would be most like her mother. She was perfect. I was flawed.

Fortunately our sex life didn't diminish the way I expected it might. Her body changed, but her desire didn't and neither did mine. We adjusted to whatever made her comfortable and managed to spend a great amount of time holding each other after sex. I believe those moments helped us deal with her disappointments and my own issues. No matter how uncertain I was about our plans, I knew spending my life with Cyn was all that mattered. I hoped she did as well.

Gregory Hedden
The Unexpected Visitor

In early March Ellen showed up at our apartment door—unannounced. Cyn had given her a standing invitation to come whenever she wanted to. Still, a phone call would have been nice. She said she was there to check on us, to make sure things were going well, but that wasn't the entire story.

Ellen put her two suitcases down by the entrance so we could hug her. After we'd greeted each other, she and Cyn walked through the kitchen to our living room and started talking. Meanwhile, I took her luggage to the spare bedroom.

It was Cyn's turn to cook. She had just started dinner but I wanted to give them time to be alone. I looked on the counter and saw a can of diced potatoes along with a package of frozen beans. She'd also been cutting up an eggplant to roast. One wouldn't be enough for the three of us and there wasn't a second in the refrigerator. I decided to put on some spaghetti. That was simple enough and would give us plenty of food. I'd still cook the eggplant so Ellen would have a choice. I stepped into the living room and offered her wine before I started to cook. I brought Cyn a Coke.

"Should I invite Bobby over?" I asked Ellen.

Ellen put her hands on her lap. "I'd love to see him again but I do have to make something clear. I have a boyfriend."

This simple statement shocked me. I thought of Ellen as someone who would never settle down with one person. Yet the tone she used when making this announcement implied she and this new man were exclusive.

"I'm only staying one night," she said. "I'm on my way to a commune near Woodstock."

This was another surprise, although one I found in keeping with my image of her.

"Commune?"

At the same time Cyn asked, "Woodstock?"

Ellen laughed. "I'll answer you both." She took in a breath. "Yes, Woodstock. Actually I'll be living in Saugerties, NY. It's near Woodstock, but along the Hudson." She smiled at Cyn then turned to me and added, "And yes, a commune." She rolled her eyes and smirked. "I have to admit this is a bit ironic. When I was at the festival with Bobby we talked about alternative ways of living. That conversation influenced my decision to go there with Sean. That's my boyfriend's name—Sean. He is one of the founding members of Libra Park."

"Libra Park?" Cyn asked.

"It's named after Sean. He's a Libra. He was born on October 22nd. That's also Timothy Leary's birthday, which is odd, since drugs are discouraged in the commune."

I sat up straight when I heard that. In a surprisingly subtle way, Ellen had just let us know about another major change in her lifestyle. She kept talking, telling us more about her new ways.

"I call it a commune but it's simply a group of people with similar backgrounds who have decided to live near each other and become a family. There are common areas but there are places that provide privacy. Anyone who can work has a job in the outside world and pays rent. The group owns the land and all the buildings."

"Is this a cult?" I asked.

Ellen's eyes narrowed. "It's a family. I hate the word cult."

I shook my head. "Sorry."

Ellen looked at Cyn and continued speaking. "Writers and artists live there. Also actors. There is a theater group with professionals and amateurs, perfect for someone like you. You could raise your child there with the help of others and continue your acting career." She turned to me. "There are colleges in that area, too. SUNY at Ulster has a physics major. I checked."

"I was just accepted at UNCG."

"So?"

"It's too late to apply somewhere else."

"That doesn't mean you can't take a year off then apply to SUNY. It's the best of all worlds for you both."

She put her palms together and touched her fingers to her lips. "There are two bedrooms available in our house, one for the two of you and one for the baby. The rent will be low. You'll have to share the kitchen and the bathroom, but only with Sean and me. If you agree, you'll be living with me, a free babysitter."

I had to admit living with a group of people who would help take care of our daughter sounded a lot better than moving in with Cyn's parents, especially since Ellen would be one of those people. I looked at Cyn and saw she was smiling.

I thought about my current plans. A gap year sounded nice. Maybe this out-of-the-blue opportunity could mean something positive for me. I asked Ellen if she would explain more of what I would be doing up there if we decided to follow her.

"Cyn says when you see something broken you always know how to fix it. If you're as good as she says, the group will cover your rent and food and pay you a little extra for other things you might need. I can't tell you how important a skill like that is in a group like this."

"You mean put off becoming a physicist to be a handyman?"

"Don't let status bother you, Gregory. People

always get too hung up on that. Just try to think about what you want and what will make your life and Cyn's life complete. All your expenses would be covered."

Ellen had a point. Taking a year off might help me understand if my dream of becoming a physicist was my own or one my parents had pushed on me. "We will have to talk it over."

"And there's no way we're heading up there before the baby's born," Cyn added.

"I thought you would say that." Ellen shifted in her chair and leaned toward Cyn. "I would never ask you to switch doctors at this late date and that's what I told Sean. He said you could talk it over. If you commit in a week or so, he'll hold the rooms until the baby's born." Ellen smiled. "I hope you'll join us. It would be great to live with you. We would see each other all the time." She turned toward me. "All of us," she added.

Living with Ellen would be wild and fun, something I might miss when our lives become a series of sleepless nights and diaper changes. I looked at Cyn, who shrugged her shoulders. She understood what I was feeling and I believed she felt the same way. "We'll talk it over," she told Ellen.

"You can call to let us know. There's a phone in the common area. You'll probably need to let it ring for a long time, but someone will answer eventually."

I nodded and then decided to change the subject. "Should I let Bobby know you're here?"

She said yes.

After dinner I made the call. Bobby said he would be over in about a half-hour. Meanwhile, Ellen stepped into the guest room to change. She'd been wearing black jeans, probably the same ones she was wearing up at Woodstock when I first met her. She'd also had on a plain navy sweatshirt and sneakers. When she came out of the guest room she was wearing a gray dress with a pattern of pink floral clusters. The dress had a high frilly collar and long sleeves with similarly frilly cuffs. The skirt came down to an inch or so above her knees, short but not what I would call a mini. She was wearing hose and black pumps. She'd also brushed her hair and pulled it back with a pink headband that matched the pattern on her dress. Her look was pretty but not overtly sexual.

Bobby arrived, wearing a black, long-sleeve shirt that was a little too tight for him. He had two of the top buttons unbuttoned. He also wore a pair of khakis and black sneakers. He had on a cologne with a slight citrus smell. I wasn't sure what brand, since I never wore scents, even aftershave. However, both Ellen and Cyn seemed to notice the aroma. Their eyes lit up when he entered the living room.

He told Ellen she looked gorgeous and hugged her until she pushed him away. The evening wasn't starting out well.

"Ellen stopped by on her way up to a commune where she's going to be living with her new boyfriend." I had explained she was in a relationship when I called Bobby but his actions seem to say he hadn't paid any attention.

He grinned and said, "Sounds as if things are going well for you."

"That's right and there's more." Ellen took a seat on the couch as she spoke. She pulled her skirt up as she crossed her legs. "Cyn and Gregory are thinking about moving to Saugerties to live next to us."

"Sounds great." Bobby took a seat in a wing chair that faced her. "I've got some good news myself. I've decided to move forward with the plan Cyn was going to use. After this semester I'm dropping out and pursuing an acting career in New York. I'll keep my apartment here in New Brunswick but go into the city every day starting in the fall."

I glanced at Cyn. Her eyes were bulging. It was clear she didn't like the idea of Bobby chasing her dream.

"That's not all," he continued. "Over the summer I'll be interning at the New Jersey Shakespeare Festival. It's at Drew University in Madison which is close enough to commute daily. I should be able to make some contacts there."

Bobby hadn't spoken to us about his plans even though we'd seen him almost daily. He must have thought Cyn would be jealous. If he did, he was right. Cyn needed theater and the community groups around Greensboro would not be enough.

"Tell Sean to save those rooms for us," I told Ellen. I looked toward Cyn. She was smiling again.

When it was time for Bobby to leave, Ellen stepped outside our apartment for a private moment with him. I'm not sure exactly what happened there but I had a feeling Ellen wasn't quite as 'exclusive' as she claimed to be.

***

When Cyn was in her eighth month, she was tired, suffering from heartburn and, in her own words, "waddling like an overstuffed walrus." All she wanted was to rest, but Bobby dropped by our apartment.

"The festival is wonderful," he told us, his eyes sparkling. "I have this sword fight with Hector in *Troilus and Cressida*. I'm just one of the unnamed soldiers who are defeated, but the scene is amazing. Personally, I think it's harder to play the man who is beaten than the victor. Anyway, the actor playing Hector comes after me swinging his sword and I have to parry. That's the word for blocking your opponent's sword with your own. You should see his expressions. I can feel his aggression and at the same time, his fear. It's a short scene, but a remarkable one."

Cyn's lips were tight. I could tell she was upset, but she answered sweetly, "I'm glad you're doing well."

I was pleased the decision to move to Saugerties had been made.

"You're right. I'm doing *very* well," he replied, seemingly oblivious to Cyn's expression. "I'm also in a production of *Treasure Island,* a Saturday matinee for kids. I play Smollett, the sea captain who fights with Long John Silver. I bought you tickets for this weekend."

"You haven't asked about Cyn's pregnancy," I pointed out as I felt the tightness in my chest start to grow. "She's due in less than a month now."

"Oh yes," he said, turning to Cyn. "How are you doing?"

"I'm tired all the time." Cyn leaned back on the couch where she was sitting and sighed.

"I hope you still want to go to *Treasure Island.* I wanted you to see me on stage."

I noticed Cyn's jaw clenching, but she said, "We'll go."

Bobby stayed for dinner that night. We walked to a Blimpie sub shop but took our sandwiches back to the apartment to eat together. Cyn and I listened as Bobby continued to babble about the Shakespeare festival. By the time he left I could tell Cyn didn't want to see him on stage, but we'd made a commitment.

The next Saturday afternoon we drove to Madison to see *Treasure Island.* I could feel Cyn's pain every time Bobby stepped on stage or when the preteen girls in the row in front of us gossiped and giggled about how handsome he was. We stayed long enough after the show to meet Bobby and compliment him. He wanted to go out with us to a bar in Madison, but we turned him down and headed home.

"I don't want to be jealous," Cyn told me as we headed south on 287.

"It's part of being human."

"I'm starting to resent our child," she said, her voice

shaking.

"Everything will be different when she arrives," I reassured her. I was also certain moving to the commune would help. Cyn needed to get away from New York theater and to be near Ellen. But we couldn't leave New Brunswick until after the birth. We trusted her doctor, who had been with her since she moved to New Jersey. Besides, making the long drive to Saugerties in such a late state of Cyn's pregnancy would make us as crazy as those young women who gave birth at Woodstock.

Gregory Hedden
Birth and Marriage

We were three days from Cyn's due date when her contractions began. We had decided I should keep up with my classes until the last minute, so I was attending a Mechanics and Waves lecture. I looked at my pager when it went off. Cyn had sent me the code we had established which meant, "Come straight home. Don't call."

I had told all my professors my girlfriend was pregnant and might have to contact me during a class. Dr. Fox had said everything was fine as long as I kept up with the classwork. When I did stand to leave during her lecture, she nodded in my direction and gave me a thumbs-up, which surprised me. All my other professors were men. I suppose I was lucky I was in Dr. Fox's class when Cyn paged. Dr. Fox turned back to the blackboard and continued writing the formula she was explaining.

When I reached our apartment, Cyn was sitting in our living room waiting for me, her suitcases by her side. I asked if the contractions were still occurring and she said they were. "They're still seven minutes apart. We should wait a little longer." I was breathing hard from my nerves and having to rush home, but I was glad Cyn had called. I wanted to be by her side.

The nurses had told us to wait until the contractions were five minutes apart, each one lasting at least one minute. That process had to continue uninterrupted for one hour. "I'll help you time them," I said, glancing at the digital alarm clock she'd placed on the coffee table, "but I'll use my watch. It has a second hand."

Cyn leaned toward me. "Spoken like a true physics major." There was some sarcasm in her tone.

I smiled. "Theater majors worry about accurate time, too."

Cyn's eyebrows went up suddenly. She wrapped her arms around her stomach. "Here comes another."

I looked at my watch and jotted down the time.

I kept monitoring Cyn until her contractions indicated it was time to go. I picked up the suitcases. We drove to the hospital in fifteen minutes. Cyn was not comfortable. She was squirming about in the passenger seat yet it was *my* heart that was beating so fast it felt as if it was about to break out of my chest.

The check-in worked well since we'd prefilled the paperwork. They took her to a labor room and I followed. A nurse looked at her and said she was beginning to dilate. These were not Braxton Hicks.

Her labor continued in a normal fashion. I was determined to be her slave for as long as it took to produce our child. That was my only goal. She asked for ice chips, I gave her ice chips. She asked me to get her a magazine, I ran to the hospital gift shop to find one.

"Do you like Bonnie?" Cyn asked when I returned with copies of *Time* and *Cosmopolitan*. I set them down on the table by her bed but I doubted she would read them.

I shrugged. "Bonnie who?" I asked.

"As a name for our daughter."

"It's nice but old-fashion. I thought we'd settled on Faye."

"We had but I'm having second thoughts."

I picked up one of the magazines and opened it to the contributor page. "There's a Charlotte here and a Molly and a Belinda. How about Belinda? I like the sound of that."

"Maybe," she said, her voice trailing off. Then she asked, "Would you rub my back?"

"Another contraction?"

"No. Just a little sore. It's probably from lying in

one position for so long."

"You want to get up, walk around a bit?"

She shook her head. "I don't think I'm supposed to." She squirmed about on the bed. "But the backrub would be nice."

I found the tennis ball we'd packed with the other things she wanted at the hospital and used it to give her the best backrub a woman in labor could have. Her gown opened in the back, which helped. A backrub with a ball was something we'd practiced in Lamaze. I liked that class. It taught us what was going on inside Cyn and helped me feel a part of the process, especially when we were doing the breathing exercises. I think her favorite part was meeting other pregnant mothers and comparing notes.

Cyn arched her back. "That's enough." I stopped and she said, "Thank you."

That was sweet. I hadn't expected her to be polite when going through so much pain. I sat back in the chair next to her bed and picked up the magazine again.

"There's an article on Theodore Roosevelt here. His mother's name was Martha and his wife was Edith."

She shook her head again. "Talk about old-fashion names."

"He had two sisters—Anna and Corinne. I like both of those."

Cyn sat up straight, her eyes bright. "I do, too, especially Corinne. It's pretty and exotic. We should think about it."

I leaned forward and took her hand. "It starts with a C. If that's our choice there will be two C. Hedden's in my life. I like that."

She laughed, but not for long because another contraction came.

Cyn was in labor for about seven hours before we moved to the delivery room. Once there I became lost in the magic of what was happening. I stood behind her, rubbing her shoulders and whispering in her ear, alternating between, "You're doing great," and, "I love you." She needed to know I was there, supporting her through this process.

I felt the tension in her body and I could see what was happening in a mirror placed in the room so the mothers could see themselves giving birth. The baby had started to crown then all at once she burst out into the doctor's arms. I could feel my heart racing at the sight of my daughter—my Corinne.

The doctor handed her to a nurse who held her while he cut the umbilical cord. She was alive. She was breathing. There was no lifting her up by her feet and smacking her bottom like I'd seen in pictures. They just cleaned her up and brought her back to her mother while the doctor dealt with the afterbirth and made sure Cyn was all right.

Corinne was a little pink body wrapped in a blanket, lying on her mother's chest, breathing evenly. I reached over and lightly touched the back of my child's head. I was in awe. Cyn and I had created a life, a wonderful, marvelous little baby girl! We'd mixed our souls together with our love and brought about this miracle! I had two loves in my life now and I would adore them both forever.

Since there were no complications Cyn and Corinne were released after two days. My mom stayed with us for a week to give Cyn time to rest and recover. Cyn's own parents didn't come to New Jersey. They didn't say why but I believe they were upset that we still weren't married.

***

Two weeks later Ellen was on the phone with Cyn, explaining how she was organizing a wedding ceremony for us at the commune. After talking for nearly an hour Cyn handed me the phone so Ellen could explain something she called a minor complication.

"It will be a spectacular celebration," she promised,

"but there won't be a minister or Justice of the Peace or anyone else like that. I will be presiding. If you and Cyn want to be legally married I suggest you get the license and visit your local courthouse before you head up this way."

I put my hand over the phone and looked at Cyn. "Is this what you want?"

She nodded. I was okay with it if she was.

That's why the first part of our wedding was at the courthouse in New Brunswick with Corinne in Cyn's arms and Bobby as our legal witness. After that procedure was done we drove to Saugerties to live with Ellen and her boyfriend, Sean.

Ellen had everything so well planned we could have held the ceremony the day after we arrived but Cyn and I both wanted our parents to attend. Mine were flexible since they planned to drive. Cyn's parents were coming from North Carolina and needed more time, causing us to wait a couple of weeks. We agreed this didn't matter. We were legal and sleeping in the same bed with Corinne in a crib beside us. To me, this was heaven. The festivities could wait.

When I first heard some of Ellen's ideas for the ceremony I was excited. She wanted a spiritual feel influenced by different religions, not narrow in its scope. In a way it reminded me of the Woodstock spirit, a sense of peace and joy yet also bordering on outrageous.

I started to worry when I saw what Ellen had decided I should wear. It was a gold, ankle-length robe with sleeves that belled out at my wrists. It had been designed by Ellen and sewn by another woman who lived in the commune two houses down from ours. It had subtle white leaf patterns throughout with green highlights bordering the collar and decorating a horizontal line about two-thirds down from my waist. The red, green and gold coloring had a Christmas feel which seemed strange for summertime.

"I'll stand out like a two-headed goat," I

complained to Cyn after Ellen went into her bedroom to give us some privacy. We were in the living room of the house we now shared with her.

"You're supposed to stand out at your wedding," Cyn told me. I noticed she was smirking.

"Not that way." I felt my stomach turn. "What will you be wearing?"

"A dress, not a robe. I can't say more than that."

"Why not?"

"You're supposed to wait until the ceremony to see my outfit. Having it described to you would be cheating."

I shifted on my feet, stepped to the couch and sat down. "If you'll be wearing a dress, why does she want me in that robe?"

"So our colors match."

"Really?" My body felt heavy. I reached up and rubbed the back of my neck. "What color is your dress?"

She raised her eyebrows and tilted her head.

"All right." I knew she wasn't going to tell me more. "The colors of the robe she wants me to wear are gold with green and red trim. I could rent a tux. Gold is out of the question. I'd look like an Elvis impersonator—and red would be a little too gaudy for my taste. But green would work, dark green. Think she would go for that?"

"Maybe." Cyn sighed. "Other than you, Ellen's my best friend and this ceremony is as important to her as it is to us. I don't want to let her down but I understand what you're saying. I've got an idea. We could both come out in matching robes then drop them to reveal my dress and your tux. Would that be okay with you?"

I shrugged. "We'll look like prize fighters at the start of a match but I guess I could live with it."

Cyn laughed. "I bet Ellen will love the drama."

***

On the day of our wedding our house was set for the ceremony. The living room couch and side chairs had been moved to the wall on the street side. The coffee table and one of the end tables were stored in our bedroom. The second end table was placed where Cyn and I would be standing. We would use it for the ceremony. Folding chairs had been brought in until there were three rows of seven and a front row of five. Counting the folding seats as well as the upholstered chairs and the couch, we had room for thirty-one. Ellen told us thirty-one was a spiritual number connected to a Hebrew name for God. However, a few people didn't show up when the wedding took place so our final number was twenty-eight. I'm not sure that was a good sign.

We invited the people who had been with us at Woodstock: Linda, Patricia, Tim, and Bobby. Only Bobby accepted. He sat on the front row along with my parents and Cyn's parents. He said he was honored. I think his experience as an actor made him love being at the front of the show.

Cyn and I entered the room and moved to the area designated for our ceremony. Ellen and Sean followed us in. They were dressed in black. They stood behind us and removed our gold robes. This was the first time I saw the dress. It was green with gold lace covering her arms, shoulders and upper chest. I was supposed to be standing next to her, standing still while looking out at our friends. But I turned my head a couple of times. I couldn't help looking at her. Cyn wasn't simply beautiful, she was like a flame lit by God.

I learned later her dress had been purchased but the gold lace and trim were added. There was a pattern throughout the entire dress, similar to the patterns in our robes. Ellen must have spent a great deal of time shopping for the right robe material to match the dress. The skirt was floor length with a slit that came up above Cyn's left knee. She wore her hair down and free with some pulled back in a loose, waterfall braid. Her look was soft magic.

The green of her dress went well with the dark green of my tux and the red of her hair matched my bowtie. Her ivory skin was like the whites of my eyes which were as wide open as possible. I was the frame while Cyn was the work of art but I was happy with that role. Happy to surround this beautiful woman forever.

We turned toward each other and bowed. Sean held a bowl of water in front of me. I washed my hands in it. When I was done he passed it to Ellen who held it in front of Cyn. She copied my motions by washing her hands while Sean handed me a towel to dry mine. When Cyn was done, Ellen handed the bowl back to Sean and picked up a towel for Cyn to use. We did this three times each.

When we were done with the ceremonial washing, we knelt on either side of the small end table. Ellen and Sean gave us each a cup. We both drank. Then they each handed us bread which we ate.

I stood. Sean gave me a small pair of scissors. I stepped behind Cyn and cut off a lock of her hair. I handed the hair and scissors back to Sean and knelt again at my side of the table. Now Cyn stood. Sean handed the scissors to Ellen who passed them to Cyn. She moved behind me and cut a lock from my hair. Ellen took both locks. Sean stepped back as Ellen tied the two locks together with a ribbon and placed them in a small silk purse for us to keep.

There was a bounce in Ellen's step as she moved forward to address the wedding guests. She took a breath and said, "As most of you know I've studied religions and spiritual beliefs from across our world. I found most religions give us something of value. But there are also aspects of some beliefs that give me pause. For example, the Greeks believed certain gods lived within Mount Olympus and people of the Judeo-Christian tradition once believed heaven existed in the clouds. Over time both of those beliefs were proven wrong.

"Among many who believe our souls live multiple

lives, there is also a belief that the souls we know in our present incarnation are always with us. For years I found this concept too convenient. Of everything we have in this life, losing our friends and families would hurt the most. So have we come up with this idea to feel better about starting over? I might believe this if it wasn't for what I see in Cyn and Gregory.

"As someone who knows these two well, I can tell you their souls pull together with a force as strong as the gravity that holds the moon in orbit. I can't even imagine a life where they aren't side by side. Grass needs soil to grow, then it decomposes and turns into nutrients within that soil. When I look at Gregory and Cyn, I can see they are like grass and soil. They need each other to exist in their best form and their marriage will help them grow together to become even closer. Cyn will grow within Gregory and Gregory will grow within Cyn. This day marks the beginning of that miracle.

"What their example means for all of us, whether we believe in reincarnation or the promise of the resurrection, is that our souls are eternal and so is our love. We can believe this because we can see it in Cyn and Gregory."

Ellen laughed a gentle, joyful laugh, then turned to go back beside Sean. When she was in place, Cyn and I leaned toward each other, across the table, and kissed. We were now married in every way possible.

We had some snacks after the ceremony: wine, beer, cookies, cheese and crackers, shrimp with cocktail sauce, cucumber canapes, stuffed mushrooms, and bean dip. It was quite a spread.

The reception provided us with a chance to talk to the people we would be living with. We'd met a few briefly, but we'd been so busy with the wedding preparations we had few chances to say anything other than, "Nice to meet you," to anybody other than Ellen and

Sean. There was the lady who had helped sew Cyn's dress and the robes. There were a few people who had helped prepare the hors d'oeuvres. There was also someone who lived in the music house. She taught piano and voice. Cyn wanted to get to know her.

This was the first time our parents had met each other. They seemed to get along well. However, none of them enjoyed the ceremony. My dad was quiet, which was unusual for him. My mother kept harping on her desire that I go back to college and finish my degree. Cyn's father objected to serving alcohol and her mother said, "I can't believe they offered you communion and didn't mention Jesus."

"It was water in those cups," Cyn told her, "not wine."

She rolled her eyes. "It seemed sacrilegious to me."

There were no spoken vows in Ellen's celebration but that night Cyn and I stood on either side of Corinne's crib and faced each other. She leaned over the crib to touch our child and I could see the tops of her breasts through the gold lace of her dress. A shiver ran up my spine. I wanted to feel her body, to hold her next to me.

"This is our beginning," I told her.

"No. This is so much more." She still had her hand on Corinne's back but she had tilted her head to look in my eyes. "Our beginning was at Woodstock. We are a family now, more than anything we could have been alone."

"Can I hug you?" I asked, stepping around the crib before she could answer.

We held each other and kissed with the same passion we'd felt on the day we conceived our daughter. I brushed Cyn's hair off her shoulder so I could move my lips down and kiss her neck.

I didn't want to let her go but she stepped away whispering, "Help me out of this dress." She faced away and I began with her braid, gently pulling off the hairband

and carefully undoing the weave. After that there were buttons on the lace covering her shoulders and a zipper below those.

As Cyn stepped out of her dress and pulled off her pantyhose I took off my jacket, tie, pants, and dress shirt. We paused for a moment to look at each other in our underclothes. She was beautiful in her strapless, low-cut bra and white panties. She seemed to be admiring me as much as I was admiring her but we still rushed to rid ourselves of the rest of our clothing.

Once we were naked we took a moment to look. We'd been together for months now. I'd worshiped her body and watched our child emerge from within her. I knew every intimate part of her, every tiny bit of her skin. I even loved the smell of her morning breath and the sweat on her body after exercise. There was nothing I didn't know and love about Cyn, yet this was all new. We were married. We had pledged our love. We were one in ways that nothing else could match.

We hugged again. We kissed again. And we made love again.

***

Our parents came back in the morning, to say goodbye to us. Each of them wanted to hold Corinne one more time but they all seemed eager to head home. I believe the general consensus among the previous generation was that the decisions we were making would lead to unhappy lives for both of us. They were right about the unhappiness but wrong about the reason.

Gregory Hedden
On Stage Again

Sean wanted Cyn to start acting right away but it took us a while to settle in, especially since Corinne was still an infant. Also, Cyn wanted to take some time to get back in shape. She established a routine including calisthenics, jogging, and swimming at the Saugerties Village Beach.

She had lost most of the baby weight when her water broke. What was actually fat, she took off quickly. She was back to looking like the Cyn I'd met at Woodstock in less than a month.

She auditioned for Sean's group on the first day of September and was immediately cast in the chorus of *Hairspray*. After that show she was in many productions including small roles in *Driving Miss Daisy* and *Come Blow Your Horn*. She was chosen to play Eliza Doolittle in *My Fair Lady*, a role that got her great acclaim. But the one that blew me away the most was *Gypsy*. Cyn played the title role, Gypsy Rose Lee, the famous stripper from the nineteen-thirties.

Cyn sang the song *Let Me Entertain You* at the climax of the story. Gypsy was pushed out on stage by her demanding mother and told to strip, but also told "…remember you are a lady." During this song the set was changed over and over as Gypsy Rose Lee gained fame and moved from club to club, each one more fancy. Cyn was fabulous at portraying Gypsy as she progressed from a nervous and somewhat shy young lady to a sophisticated woman who discovers she loves the attention she receives.

Meanwhile I took care of Corinne. I understand why many young mothers feel lonely and separated from the real world, but living in a commune is different. Ellen was always around and there were others as well. There were people willing to share a bottle of wine with me after I'd put Corinne down for the night or watch her while I read a book.

Cyn wanted to take over completely when she was between shows or had a night off. I agreed to step back even though I still enjoyed the routine of tending to a baby.

I could tell from watching them how difficult it was for Cyn to keep close to Corinne while maintaining her passion for performing. Both those parts of her life were important to her. Only time would tell how well she could balance them.

St. Joseph's Oratory
On the Steps #2

They paused to take a break. Gregory was exhausted from the little bit of climbing they had accomplished. They looked around to see the other pilgrims. Corinne and Gregory seemed to be the only two who were climbing as a pair. Corinne was helping Gregory as much as she could, but she couldn't carry him. For this to work, Gregory had to manage the steps under his own power.

There was a man a few steps ahead of them, dressed in a gray short sleeve sweatshirt and dark jeans. His left leg was missing but he still had two knees to crawl on. His pants leg was pinned. Gregory leaned over to his daughter and whispered, "It would be one hell of a miracle if that guy's leg grows back."

"God can do anything," Corinne told him.

He rubbed his neck. "I suppose so. Miracles are God's way of building bridges to wherever He wants us to go."

Corinne smiled. "I just hope He hears our prayers."

"How will God see past that unfortunate man to find me? With one leg gone, he has to be working twice as hard to climb these steps."

"God can see the injuries you carry inside."

A woman was on her knees a few steps ahead of the one-legged man. She was wearing a long robe and a hijab. She was dressed like a Muslim yet she was at St Joseph's, praying to a Catholic saint.

"What do you think of her?" Gregory asked. "She seems out of place, doesn't she?"

"These steps are holy. People come from all over

the world to pray here. In the end their prayers help us as much as our prayers help them."

Corinne and Gregory each said one of those prayers, then started to climb, kiss, and pray again. Gregory included the man with one foot and the woman wearing the hijab in his. All of God's flock deserved compassion.

***

They hadn't planned their trip with the weather in mind but the beautiful June day couldn't have been better if it had been designed for a Broadway show about heaven. The temperature was in the low 70s. A few cumulus clouds were blowing across a blue sky. Gregory had on a Yankees ball cap to keep his scalp from burning. His hair was gone now, due to his chemo treatments. Other than that, they were dressed in similar outfits. They both were wearing short sleeve T-shirts, Gregory's gray and Corinne's green. They also were wearing jeans and sneakers. Unlike the Arab woman ahead of them, they were dressed for climbing.

Gregory glanced over his shoulder. The view was a magnificent canvas covered with the colors of the Notre Dame buildings and the other smaller structures that surrounded the college. He was grateful to see this beauty, almost enough to make him forget about the pain he was feeling.

He took a deep breath and drifted back into his memories. Those thoughts gave him the strength to keep on climbing, kissing, and praying.

***

Corinne's belief in her father's love was surrounded by a shell of guilt. His presence gave her hope but it wasn't enough to break that shell.

"I never could understand how you could love me after Mom died," she told him, "and now my sacrilege has hurt you as well."

"How could I love you?" Gregory said, repeating and questioning her words. He grimaced. "How could I not?"

Corinne covered her face with her hands and spoke through them. She couldn't look at her father. "I'm not only responsible for what happened to Mom but for what's happening to you. I betrayed God when I should have been worshipping Him!"

"You are here showing the strength of your faith," Gregory told her in a steady, low voice. "Let's keep climbing."

***

Gregory's right shoulder began to itch. He was climbing on his knees and using his hands like the front legs of an animal. He twisted around and sat up.

Corinne narrowed her eyes. "What is it?"

"I feel a sudden itch on my shoulder. It's unbearable."

"Can you scratch it?"

"Yes, but it's moved to my neck. It feels like a colony of ants making their way down my back."

"That's horrible. Do you need my help?"

"No...no...I'm okay, I guess. The ants are starting to fade, only now there's a sharp pain in my stomach." His voice tightened from the torment. "I've felt this before, but it is so much worse this time."

Corinne moved behind her father. "Let me rub your shoulders," she said, placing her hands on him. "You just sit there and breathe easy. Maybe you're scared and that's what's bringing this on?"

"No...it's real. Oh my God. Stomach pain is a side effect but I never...oh...ouch."

Gregory took in a sharp breath, then suddenly stopped squirming. He remembered the day when Cyn gave birth to Corinne and thought how death and birth were both surrounded by pain.

He looked into Corinne's eyes. "What did you say?" His voice was normal.

"I didn't say anything. I'm too scared."

"I heard your voice. You said, 'Come to me.'"

"I didn't say that." She was trembling. "Are you okay?"

"I think so."

Corinne leaned toward her father and hugged him.

"The itching and the pain, all of it went away as suddenly as it came. I don't understand any of this," he told her.

"Maybe God was speaking to you," she suggested.

Gregory shook his head slowly. "Or maybe it was your mother's voice."

Corinne had heard her mother's voice before. What her father was saying was possible. "Mom said 'Come to me?' What could that mean?"

"I think she wants us to start climbing again."

"Are you able to do that?"

"The itching and pain are gone. It's as if none of that happened."

Corinne hugged him again and grinned. "Then we should go on."

They repeated their prayers, kissed the next step and resumed the climb.

***

"Your mom's words are ambiguous," Gregory said the next time they stopped for a rest. "How do I go to her? Am I supposed to keep climbing or am I supposed to leave?"

Corinne rubbed her eyebrows. "I think that's pretty clear. Mom never spoke to you before you were climbing these steps and now she says 'Come to me?' She has to be telling you to keep climbing."

"But how do we know?" Gregory was now certain the voice he'd heard was Cyn's, but this was a fork in their road. He didn't want the pain of the struggle to influence his decision either way. Corinne had some logic on her side, but maybe Cyn spoke up because he was doing the wrong thing.

Corinne saw her father frown. "You have to decide what makes the most sense and keep with your decision," she told him, hoping she wouldn't lose him now.

"You're saying I shouldn't give up just because we've come so far?"

"If this wasn't right, Mom would have contacted you before we got here. Her words have to be an encouragement. She must be waiting for us at the top of these stairs."

Gregory sighed. "Alright. Let's keep moving."

***

"Can we stop?" Gregory asked after four more steps.

"Of course. Are you hurting again?"

"No," he told her, but he knew the pain could come out of nowhere, like a lightning strike on a clear day. "I'm just tired."

"We'll rest some more."

They were slow but still moving in the right direction.

Gregory pressed his lips together. "I can't give up now that your mother is calling."

Corinne shook her head slowly. "When I was five years old and heard her voice for the first time I knew immediately it was Mom. That wasn't true for you, right?"

"I thought it was you at first, but that's because you're so much like your mom."

Corinne scratched the back of her neck and said, "When I heard her voice it was never the sound I recognized. It was something else, a sensation that hit my brain and made me remember all these small things about her: her smell, the intonations in her speech, the way her arms felt when she hugged me."

"Yes," Gregory said, feeling a lightness in his chest. "What I experienced was like that, sensations throughout my body and every one speaking to me, reminding me of your mom." He looked Corinne straight in her eyes. "It was your mom. I'm certain."

***

They had lost count, but Corinne was sure they were approaching the halfway mark. Her father, who had always been a pillar of strength, was out of breath. He was panting again. They needed another break.

They were on their knees, so they both turned over and sat on the step. "You need to rest for a while." Corinne wanted to reach for her dad, to hold him, but she kept her hands on her lap. "When the pain passes we can move on."

Gregory smiled. "Sometimes pain is good." He flinched, as he went on to explain. "Mine teaches me about myself and about the people I have loved throughout my life."

"You mean Mom, right?"

"I'm talking about you. I knew every part of your mom from her red hair and pale skin through the depths of her soul." He closed his eyes and smiled. "You, however, have often fooled me. This trip, this experiment with God's miracles, seemed at first to be your solution to my cancer. I suppose it is, but it's also a reaction to your guilt. I wish I'd seen that in you earlier. I would have told you how misguided it is."

"It's not," she said in a low voice, speaking more to herself than to him. "If it wasn't for me Mom would be alive today."

Corinne Hedden
Buttermilk Falls

I have memories from the time before the waterfall: my mom showing me how to peel potatoes and mash them in an old-fashioned masher, her sitting on the side of my bed while she read Winnie the Pooh stories, me playing in a sandbox with Mom and Aunt Ellen, and sleeping in Mom's old room when we visited my grandparents in North Carolina.

My dad took me to see her in a play when I was four, the first time I saw her act. I remember squirming a lot since I was so young, but I'm glad he took me. I remember the play as clearly as any other memory from my childhood. Mom played a dancer with her own studio, so I saw her dance on the commune stage. I watched her spin around, her black skirt billowing out in waves.

Uncle Sean was in the show with her. They talked a lot on the stage, sitting at a small table, drinking coffee. Their characters went to a party where Mom had to act as if she drank too much alcohol. Uncle Sean had to carry her because she couldn't walk. He took her across the stage where her apartment was set up and put her to bed. He had to struggle with her to get her coat off.

To me Mom wasn't a character in a play. She was my mother and I felt bad she was with Uncle Sean instead of my dad. Still Dad wasn't upset. His eyes were on her every move and he was smiling.

After the show Mom and Uncle Sean talked to some people in the audience. Uncle Sean spent most of his time with Aunt Ellen, while Mom came to me and Dad. He hugged her then she hugged me. Mom hugged me all the time, but I remember how my skin tingled at her touch that day.

"Did you enjoy the show?" she asked me, kneeling down to put her face right in front of mine.

I nodded. I wish I had said more about how much fun it was watching her on that stage, but I was shy. I held her hand while we talked to other people. All of our friends from the commune were there.

It was a wonderful life, but the following year everything changed at Buttermilk Falls.

***

The falls have a dangerous beauty. There are multiple drops, some with single, long descents while others have rock steps splitting the stream of water in many places. All of the drops are surrounded by forests of pine, oak, and maple among others. Many of the rocks near the water are covered in moss which looks gorgeous but is slippery and treacherous. The sun often shines through the trees and if the light falls right the scene can be magical.

Even though the forest blocked much of the sun, my mom was wearing her outdoor clothing: sunglasses, a straw hat, a white, long sleeve blouse, and a yellow, maxi skirt.

Aunt Ellen was with us that day. She's the one who first saw the small herd of deer in the woods. The animals drew their attention which is why they didn't notice when I wandered off toward the falls. I don't know why I wasn't interested in the deer. I suppose I was enthralled by the sound of the water running over stones. While they looked for the animals hiding amongst the trees, I walked toward the Raquette River.

When they discovered I was missing, my mother ran toward the falls. I learned later that Dad and Aunt Ellen also looked for me but not toward the water. They started off along a path through the woods.

When my mom reached the edge of the river at the waterfall, I had already crawled out onto one of the stones.

I told her I was looking for a rainbow.

"Stay where you are!" Mom shouted. She looked upstream and downstream before focusing on the rocks that led out to me. I could see her hands shaking as she took off her shoes. She managed to step onto the first stone, but without her shoes the skirt dragged and the rushing water caught its hem. She lifted the material to her knees.

She took four or five steps, then slipped. She fell, hitting her head on a stone and rolling into the current. Mom was washed down the waterfall, banging into stone after stone until she reached the bottom.

"Mommy!" I yelled. "Mommy!"

Then I started screaming sounds that made no sense, just loud shrieks. I looked down the falls and wanted to go after her but I was scared. My legs were weak and I had to kneel on the rock where I had been standing. I started to cry. I tried to yell again but I still couldn't form the words.

Aunt Ellen and Dad came running from the woods. He looked down the falls and started yelling even louder than I had. "Cyn!" he cried out. "Cyn! Cyn!"

He climbed down the stones along the side of the waterfall while Aunt Ellen came out on the rocks to reach me. She took my hand and brought me back. When I was on solid land I looked down again. Mom's skirt had caught on what appeared to be a tree branch stuck among the rocks. It had been ripped off and was now waving above her like a warning flag. She lay on rocks at the bottom, the white skin on her legs, her stomach, her arms and face all stained with red blood.

By the time Dad reached her she was dead. I didn't know that at the time, but I did hear him wail and watched as he wrapped his arms around her and buried his head on her chest, the river water splashing around them both. That was over thirty years ago, but whenever I think about that day I still see him holding onto her red and white body with yellow material blowing in the wind above them and I know she wouldn't have died if I hadn't been chasing a rainbow.

***

A few weeks after the accident Aunt Ellen tried to ease my pain by taking me back to the park with the sandbox. She filled one of my toy buckets from a nearby fountain and used the water to make the sand easier to mold. She sat with me and began to build. We made a walled city. I managed a few houses that were good enough to recognize as something other than mounds of sand, but Aunt Ellen built an elaborate church, complete with a bell-tower.

I don't suppose it takes much to impress a five-year-old child, but I remember it as an amazing sculpture—and not just because of the way it looked. There was a presence inside that sand church, one that confused me. I knew the presence was a woman even though I could not see her. I could understand what she was telling me. I could feel it in my head and heart.

She said, "Sing and dance," which was odd because she was asking me to do something I did all the time. I'd been singing since I'd first learned *Twinkle Twinkle Little Star* and I sang along with the radio, especially with the Jackson Five, my favorite group. I also loved to dance. I would spin around the living room we shared with everyone in the commune until I was dizzy. I liked it when others would watch me dance.

I never forgot the voice that came from the sand church.

***

At first I missed my mom and felt so guilty over my role in her death I couldn't even say her name. For a while Dad gave me the space I needed, perhaps because he needed the same thing. Then, after a month or so had passed he came to me in my room and sat on the edge of my bed the way Mom used to when she read to me.

"We need to talk," he said, his eyes tearing up.

"Why?"

"Because we're both crying inside and that's worse than crying outside."

"Is it?"

"It keeps us from healing."

He looked down at his hands and back at me. "Did you know your mom and I met at a magical place?"

"Magic?"

"It was a music festival called Woodstock. I was sitting among thousands of people in a field with a huge stage at the bottom of a hill where musicians were playing so loudly you could hear their songs for miles."

"More people than on meeting day?" On Thursdays everyone in the commune got together to talk about problems. I was too small to know about the problems, but not too small to enjoy having all the people I lived with in one room.

"So many more. More even than all the people living in Saugerties. Yet, out of all those people, your mother and I met. I was sitting on the hill watching the musicians and listening to their music when she walked by. I knew I loved her as soon as I saw her."

"Like in Cinderella?" The commune had a copy of the Disney film and it was my favorite.

"Yes, very much like Cinderella, because your mom left in a hurry without telling me how we could get in touch. I had to search for her, just like the prince looked for Cinderella in the movie."

"And you found her?"

"Yes I did and we had a baby together. That baby was you."

I smiled, but we were both quiet until I said, "I miss her."

My dad slowly blew out his cheeks and said, "Of course you do." He touched my shoulder.

I thought of the voice from the sand church and spoke softly saying, "She wants me to sing and dance. If she was here she could teach me."

"You do both of those things beautifully."

My dad hugged me. He couldn't bring my mom back, but I'd gotten to him. He thought of a way he could honor my wish.

"If you want to learn how professionals sing and dance," he told me, squeezing my hand, "I know someone who might be able to help."

When Dad made that suggestion, I didn't realize he was talking about Bobby. Bobby's career had been going well. He wasn't someone I would call famous, but he'd been on Broadway in the original cast of *A Little Night Music*. He'd also been in a touring company of *Applause*. He was more than qualified to teach me and, many years later, his success would turn out to be important to my own.

Gregory Hedden
Mourning and Moving On

After the accident I cried every day. My body often shook and my limbs felt weak. I could hardly stand, yet when I went to bed I couldn't sleep. For weeks I felt as if I was being waterboarded under the waterfall that had killed her.

I sat with Corinne and held her, rocking and crying with her. I had to do that. I tucked her in bed every night. I had to let her know I was still there for her, but Ellen took care of the day-to-day necessities. She washed our clothes and prepared our meals. After a week had passed, she took on the tasks of making sure Corinne was dressed properly, packing her lunch and driving her to school every day.

I notified Cyn's parents the day after the accident. They weren't home when I called so I left a message saying, "This is Gregory. Please call me as soon as you get this." It was another couple of hours before they learned what had happened.

When I told them I had trouble speaking and when I finally got the words out her father couldn't say anything, but Cyn's mother shouted, "Leave her where she is!" I expected her to be upset but she sounded angry. "Don't do anything else! We will handle it from here!"

An ambulance had taken her body to a funeral home in Saugerties. Cyn's parents wanted to have her taken to North Carolina. Since I was the next of kin they had to call me back and ask for my permission. I gave it and signed the necessary paperwork. I have no idea how much they paid to have her transported to Greensboro but that's what they did. They had a funeral for her at their church and Cyn was buried in a plot they already owned. The only reason I knew all of this was they informed Ellen of their plans.

They had known Ellen since Cyn and she were children. I guess that counted more to them than the fact that I was her husband.

Cyn's mother wrote an obituary that was published in the Greensboro paper. I wrote one that was published in the Saugerties Times. I was mentioned in theirs and they were mentioned in mine. Other than that, they were very different tributes. The one in North Carolina focused on her membership in the Baptist church and about her life from birth through high school. The one I wrote spoke more about her acting, singing, and dancing. Both obituaries referred to her as a wonderful, loving mother, although mine said wife and mother.

If I'd had my way I suppose I would have had her cremated and had her ashes either scattered in Bethel at the festival site or placed under a tree in our yard in Saugerties. I gave in to the request to bury Cyn in Greensboro because I loved her soul, not her dead body, and I knew Cyn would not have wanted me to fight with her parents.

In the weeks that followed her mother's death, Corinne and I walked around our town every evening. We held hands and talked about Cyn's life. It was our way of mourning together, away from the well-intentioned friends we had in the commune. My young daughter was all that kept me going as the days turned to months.

***

A year after Cyn's death, Ellen approached me. "You have lost so much," she said, then she paused and took a step back. "I know you, Gregory. I know you can't move on and I know Cyn would want you to. You need to find someone else."

I felt a chill in my core. "To move on from her? Cyn was my world. I can't do that."

"If you don't you'll never be happy again."

"I have Corinne. She and I understand each other."

"She's family but she can't be enough. She's a six-year-old child."

"I have plenty of adult friends to talk to. That's one of the reasons I love living in Libra Park. We help each other through times like this."

"You know we all love you but it has been a year."

"I know that."

"Conversations are wonderful but not enough, not for someone as young and vital as you."

"Are you talking about sex?"

She nodded and looked down. She seemed as if she was embarrassed to bring up this subject. I could see why. Ellen and I were great friends. She had helped me through the hardest year of my life. We had mourned together. She had helped Corinne get through the loss of her mother. She had been with us when we needed her the most. But this? With her?

I felt my face flush because she was right. Although I had her and others to talk to and I had Corinne to take care of, I was alone physically. I had pictures of Cyn that I used to remember our most passionate times and that helped sometimes. Yet it had been so long since I'd felt the soft, smooth body of a woman next to me in bed. I wondered if sleeping with Ellen would ruin our friendship. Cyn would want me to move on, but with her best friend? I didn't know about that. There were other complications, too. I knew Ellen wouldn't give up Sean if our relationship became physical and I didn't think I could face him if we did something behind his back, even if it was only one time. Still, a warm body beside me...

Ellen lifted her head and cleared her throat. "Michelle McBride has a daughter who lives in Tivoli. She thinks the two of you would get along well."

Michelle was the seamstress who had helped sew our wedding robes and Cyn's dress. I covered my mouth with my hand. *So that's what this is about. Thank God I*

didn't answer first.
"Michelle's daughter is eager to meet you. If you agree, she can come up here or you can go to her house." Ellen smiled. "Sean and I can go with you if you're uncomfortable meeting with her alone."

"Alone will be fine, if you're available to sit with Corinne."

"Of course I am."

***

If Ellen had come right out and told me she was arranging a blind date, I probably would have turned her down. Instead, I was so relieved she wasn't asking me to change the nature of our friendship, I accepted her suggestion without giving it much thought.

I did miss sex, yet when I said that to myself, I sounded as if I wanted nothing else. That couldn't have been further from the truth. I missed my conversations with Cyn and I missed watching her when she did little things such as drinking a cup of coffee or putting on her makeup. I loved the interests we shared, the books we both read or the films we'd seen together. Cyn was my soulmate and I doubted I could ever find that connection with anyone else, but if there was someone out there, someone who could walk beside me and hold me at night, I would love to find that person.

***

I knew a few things about the woman I was about to meet. Her name was Naomi. She was twenty-five, a year younger than I was. Her mother was Japanese so the family name, McBride, came from her father. He didn't live with Naomi's mother in the commune and no one ever mentioned him. I assumed he'd either died or the marriage had not lasted.

A couple of years before this arranged date I had

asked Ellen if she knew what happened to Michelle's husband. She shook her head. "Everybody who lives here has some history. It's their right to tell or not tell. I never ask."

I let the subject drop back then, but now the missing husband/father meant that Naomi and I had both lost a family member. It was possible she didn't care or was even happy he was gone, but it was more likely she grieved his loss. If so, we shared an overwhelming emotion. It wasn't something I could bring up, especially on a first date, but it could be a connection that would lead to a deeper relationship.

Although I didn't have a picture of Naomi, her mother had told me she would be wearing a black skirt and orange crop top. I arrived at the Traghaven Whiskey Pub early and found she was already there, sitting with a friend, a blonde woman with long hair, which was a contrast to Naomi's mid-length dark hair. Naomi's friend was wearing an orange sleeveless dress with a black pattern that matched Naomi's midriff top. That couldn't have been a coincidence.

"Naomi?" I asked when I approached the table.

"You must be Gregory." She remained sitting but held out her hand for me to shake. "This is my friend Ashley. She'll be joining us but don't worry. I'll pay for her."

I didn't say anything, just tilted my head.

"You're okay with this, aren't you?" Naomi put her arm around Ashley as she smiled at me. "Because if you're not…"

I interrupted before she could tell me to leave. "I'm good." I shrugged, and sat in the booth across from the women.

Naomi put her hands up in her hair and flipped it back. "Ashley's my best friend and she's moving to Paris tomorrow. She's got a job with Girbaud. I just learned about all of this yesterday." Naomi sat up in her chair. "So here she is."

"Girbaud?" I asked, trying to roll with whatever these two had planned.

"They make jeans," Ashley said, "and other casual wear."

"Impressive."

"Not really. I'll be in finance, but I'll get a discount on their clothes and I may be able to move into fashion design later." She paused for a moment and put on a broad smile. "I know I'll love Paris. It's got to be better than Tivoli."

"But you'll miss me, right?" Naomi pleaded.

"Of course. You'll always be my buddy."

The waiter came over to take my drink order. I looked at what Naomi and Ashley were drinking. They had clear drinks with ice and lime wedges. I thought they were gin and tonics but I wasn't sure. I said, "I'll have what they have."

"No you won't," Naomi told me. "You're our designated driver. Ashley and I are getting looped tonight. You're staying sober."

I blew out my cheeks. "Okay."

I turned to the waiter and told him I'd have water with lemon. He went to get my drink.

During the date, if you could call it that, Naomi and Ashley mostly talked to each other and ignored me.

"What about the time we were flirting with those guys in Florida?" Naomi said. "Remember that?"

Ashley winced. "Of course I do. I wish I could forget it. They followed us back to our hotel."

"Yeah. That could've gone really bad but they turned out to be innocent enough."

"Still, it was scary."

Most of their stories were similar tales of trips they took together, pranks they played on other students and parties they attended. I learned they double-dated to their prom and partied with their dates after the dance at a hotel in Tannersville. Naomi had lost her virginity that night, to a guy who was not her date. Ashley reminded her of that fact and they both laughed. If either of them even remembered I was sitting there, they'd both had so much to drink they didn't care.

Although they repeatedly claimed to have always been best friends, they didn't tell stories that occurred after they graduated from high school. I had the feeling they'd gone separate ways years ago and this decision of Ashley's to move to France was just an excuse to get together one more time to reminisce.

"Do you reeemember color guard?" Naomi said, speaking slowly.

Ashley hugged her. "I shhhure do."

"I love you for that."

"That was show unfair. You were good. I'd not be part of that shhtupid thing without you. Never. Never. Never. I love you."

"I…love…you…too."

They hugged again.

Near as I could figure out, they'd tried out for color guard together and Naomi hadn't made it. They both thought it was because she was half Japanese. Ashley dropped out in protest.

I suppose Naomi's loss of her father was part of what made the loss of her good friend so hard to bear. She was dealing with this loss by drinking; they both were. I hoped this wasn't something that happened all the time, for either of these women.

When it was time to take them home I paid the check for all three of us. Naomi watched me and didn't object despite what she'd said earlier.

Ashley was spending the night at Naomi's house, so I didn't have to drop them off separately. I did have to bring them up to the porch because Ashley couldn't walk without leaning on me. Naomi opened the door and we all went inside. I left Ashley on the couch and turned to leave. Naomi followed me back to the porch.

"Shhorry 'bout tonight," she said, stumbling over her words a little less than before.

"That's all right, it was an interesting night."

"Not what you 'spected, right?"

"Not exactly."

"I have a rule." She was shaking her head. "No sex until third date but you…yoooo were a good shhhport. So tonight counts as two." She leaned against the door jam and held up two fingers. "You call me."

I smiled but didn't say I would or wouldn't. I went down the porch steps.

"Hey!" Naomi shouted. I turned and watched as she lifted her top and flashed her breasts. "You call!" She laughed as I left.

I didn't call and didn't answer her messages. A month later Michelle apologized for her daughter's behavior and told me again we would be a good match under different circumstances.

"I understand." I wondered how much about that date Naomi had told her. I still didn't contact her daughter.

Naomi had behaved much like Ellen had at Woodstock and I had loved Ellen's wild side. I'm not sure what was different this time. Maybe it was because I was older and the father of a young girl. Maybe it was because I was expecting a traditional date with Naomi. Maybe it was because Ellen was showing off while Naomi was rude. Whatever the reason, I decided I wasn't ready for the complications of dating. I had Corinne to look after and the memories of Cyn to keep me going.

Corinne Hedden
The Class

It took three years before Bobby finally came to the commune for my first lesson. I was eight. We started with dance and finished the class with singing. He played his guitar while we sang *The Walrus and the Carpenter* together.

"Acting is something we'll work on another time," he told me.

I liked when he said that. It meant he planned on coming back.

The lesson had gone on for an hour. When it was over Bobby asked me what I thought.

"It was fun, but it would be better if I had a friend with me."

"Anyone in mind?"

"My friend, Azalea." Everyone said Azalea and I looked alike, but that was mainly because we both smiled most of the time and had blonde hair. Anyone who looked closer could see she was a little chubbier than I was and her hair only came down to her shoulders. Mine reached my lower back.

"That's a good idea," Bobby told me. "There's no reason this can't be open to others and I could use the extra money. I'd like to have five or six in the class, as long as they're all as enthusiastic as you are."

No one driving past our homes would know we were a commune. Our street looked like every other block in the area, older homes built close to the road. The only aspect of the commune homes that differed from the others was the flower gardens. Every one of our houses had a garden in front or beside the building. This was due to Azalea's mother, Phyllis, who loved plants and did most of the work.

Sean lived in our house with Aunt Ellen. He and Gloria McLean, who lived across the street from us, both came from wealthy families. They had pooled their resources to purchase ten homes next to each other, four on one side of the street and six on the other. The commune was a corporation. The rent money did not go to Sean and Gloria. It went to the business and was used to cover upkeep on the buildings, including my dad's salary.

The residents of Libra Park had private bedrooms, but all the other areas were shared. It was convenient that way. If someone was preparing a meal requiring more than one oven, that person would go to the next house over and use the one there. A few sign-up lists were established for things such as the stage area where Aunt Ellen led her meditation exercises and the theater group rehearsed, but most everything else was on a first-come, first-served basis. People were encouraged to communicate often in order to prevent conflict.

***

The classes started two weeks after Bobby agreed to include my friends. We had six kids with us, me and Azalea from Libra Park and four others from my school: Amy, Jennifer, Heather, and Melissa. We were sitting in the front row of the chairs set up for the audience. Uncle Sean and Bobby were up on stage.

Uncle Sean was the first to speak. "As you know, Corinne's dad has requested that his friend Bobby Miller be allowed to teach a theater class. Bobby has been working as an actor for some years and knows many tricks. I've been in charge of the Libra Players for about the same length of time, directing as well as acting. So I'm going to join him and together we will hold this class. If you children work hard and listen to your teachers, you will be prepared when you get your chance to be in a show."

When Uncle Sean was done Bobby grinned, leaned forward and spoke. "A play I was in won a Tony for best musical. It's called *A Little Night Music*. Maybe one of you will win one someday."

Uncle Sean turned to Bobby. "They don't know what a Tony is."

Bobby furrowed his brow and turned back to the students. "A Tony is the highest award possible in theater."

"The Tony awards are as political as any other awards," Sean said to Bobby, loud enough for everyone to hear. He turned back to the kids. "Tonys are given out based on who you know rather than what you did."

Even though I was only eight, I could feel their tension growing.

"That's totally wrong. The best of the best win Tonys."

"You didn't win one. It was for the show, not for you."

"I helped make that show great."

"Maybe, maybe not."

When I had suggested inviting my friends to join our class, I hadn't expected anything like this. *Why are they fighting?*

Bobby and Uncle Sean seemed to remember kids were watching. They turned their attention back to us, smiled and seemed friendly again, which I suppose meant they were both good actors.

"We're going to split the class," Bobby told us. "Corinne, you, Azalea, and Melissa will start with Sean. Heather, you, Amy, and Jennifer will work with me. After a half-hour we'll switch."

We were only six girls, so we didn't need to be in smaller groups. Uncle Sean and Bobby probably came up with this plan so they wouldn't have to work together.

"The fancy word for what we are going to try is improvisation," Uncle Sean told us when we gathered on his side of the stage, "but pretending is a much better word. You all like to pretend, right?"

We nodded, all three of our heads bobbing up and down as if we were tied together.

"Good." He put his hands together and stood up straight. "I want you to pretend the three of you are in a swimming pool. You are about to race across the length of the pool. When you reach the far side, you climb out of the pool and react to what just happened."

"React?" I asked.

"Yes. Maybe you act proud if you won or mad if you didn't. Or maybe you didn't win, but you decide to congratulate the girl who did. Or maybe you accuse the winner of cheating. That's fine, too. When you are on stage sometimes you act in a bad way and sometimes in a good way. You have to decide what the person you are pretending to be would do, not what you would do or what your parents would expect you to do. You have to make the scene seem real."

"I don't know how to swim," Azalea told him.

"That's okay, too," Uncle Sean replied. "Like I said, pretending is what acting is about."

We lined up on one side of the stage and when Uncle Sean said "Go," we waved our arms and moved across the stage pretending we were pushing through water. Melissa got to the other side first, because she was the only one trying to go fast. When we caught up with her I said, "You're such a good swimmer."

"Thank you," she answered.

Uncle Sean stopped us. "You have to imagine you're in the pool. That means you have to either climb out or hang on the pool wall while talking to each other. Also, you need to use your bodies as well as your voices. When you congratulate Melissa you can shake her hand or even hug her."

"Do I get to win the race next time?" Azalea asked.

He laughed and said, "If you wish."

We did other scenes, too. We pretended we were talking about a party and one of us hadn't been invited. I got to be that person. Another scene was in school with Azalea pretending to cheat on a test. I let her read my paper while Melissa called the teacher and tattled on us both. This was so much fun. We loved pretending.

When the class was half over we switched to the other side of the stage and started learning dance from Bobby. We started with stretches. After those he told us to make shapes with our bodies and to move in ways we felt were comfortable and fun. "There's no right or wrong with this," he said. Some of us spun around, others did cartwheels or somersaults. We stood back to back, hooked our arms and tried to make shapes with a partner. I was with Azalea while Melissa paired with Bobby. Even though I knew Azalea so well, we still moved in opposite directions at times. We had to get used to each other. In the end, the dancing was as much fun as the pretending.

***

The class was great, but the fighting found its way back to our dinner table.

When we ate apart from the other Libra Park families, cooking was my dad's responsibility. I helped that night. We had garlic butter salmon, at least most of us at the table did. Dad became a vegetarian after Mom died. He said he did it in her honor. So after all the work he did on the fish, he ate nothing except the beans and rice I had cooked. I talked about becoming a vegetarian also, but he said I was still growing and needed protein. I would have to wait to make that choice. I was glad to wait because I liked meat. As always, Uncle Sean and Aunt Ellen ate whatever we put in front of them. Bobby also ate everything and raved about the dinner.

Once we were done eating and the adults each had a

couple of glasses of wine, Bobby and Uncle Sean started arguing again.

"Why are you two at each other's throats?" Aunt Ellen asked.

"We weren't fighting," Uncle Sean told her, "just talking about the class. Bobby had the kids creating shapes with their bodies and I don't see how that is helping them. They should be learning the basic disciplines. How to hold their arms. How to position their feet. Things like that."

Bobby's face turned red. "Look who's talking," he said to Uncle Sean before turning to speak to the rest of us. "He had the kids pretending to swim in a pool. Worse than that, they were racing. Why would he think kids could do that? They would have to lie on the stage to get close to the right movements and then they couldn't move anywhere. It's an impossible task. They ended up walking across the stage waving their arms as if they were swatting at mosquitoes."

When they stopped arguing for a moment I said, "It was a great class. We all had fun."

"I'm sure you did," Aunt Ellen told me. She looked at Uncle Sean and then at Bobby. "There's something else going on here, isn't there?"

They both seemed to slouch in their chairs. "Both of you need to come with me to our room," she told them. "We need to talk alone."

What I didn't realize at the time was the argument had more to do with Aunt Ellen than with how the class was going. Both Bobby and Uncle Sean liked Aunt Ellen enough to fight for her and that was what was happening.

***

A couple of years later when we spoke about that day she told me, "I didn't want to hear their explanations. That would have aggravated them both. Instead, I had them sit next to each other and meditate." She wiggled her nose and squinted a bit. I could tell she was enjoying telling the story. "I had them chant together, then I told them to wrap their anger and jealousy up in a package and toss it away." She laughed. "It worked. I don't know if you remember, but Bobby stayed over that night. The three of us slept in our bed with Bobby on my right and your Uncle Sean on my left. No touching, just lying there together. I don't know how well they slept, but in the morning they were cordial to each other. Maybe they'd lost the anger or maybe they were faking it. Either way they were pleasant to each other. From that time on, whenever all three of us were here at Libra Park, we all slept in one bed."

"I guess that's why they didn't argue in class anymore."

"Meditation is powerful." Aunt Ellen leaned in as she spoke. "Much more powerful than drugs. Remember that." She winked at me.

Back then I had no idea why Aunt Ellen would know about drugs, but I believed her and I learned something even more important. Aunt Ellen had to be a powerful woman to convince two men that sharing was better than fighting.

Corinne Hedden
Wind Chimes

The class went on for years. Bobby and Uncle Sean were good teachers, but we also had guest instructors who had their own ideas and tricks. Whenever Bobby had a role in a show that kept him away from us he would send a substitute from among his many connections with dancers and actors in New York. When that happened Uncle Sean would always step back and say, "You need to learn as much as possible from..." We did as we were told and all of us grew our skills, including Uncle Sean who would watch and sometimes take notes.

Azalea got to be a pretty good dancer, but not as good as me. I was the best dancer and singer in the class and everyone knew it. Azalea was best at making up the stories for our improvs and said she wanted to be a writer someday. Melissa dropped out when she was eleven but the two of us, along with Amy, Jennifer, and Heather, kept attending and a boy named Anthony joined. He was a little clumsy but very strong. We started using him to lift us.

Azalea became my best friend. I suppose that's because we both lived in the commune and saw each other all the time. Still, we felt a real connection. We shared a love of the outdoors and would often go on long walks together. When we were young we would talk about games we played and our favorite songs and about silly things like making animal noises or the best and worst smells we could think of. Azalea had been sprayed by a skunk once, so her worst smell was always that. Mine changed from time to time. We shared our favorite smell which was usually the incense Aunt Ellen burned at her meditation sessions.

As we grew older we talked more about boys.

Mostly about boys we didn't know, but we liked to look at in school. We hadn't talked about our favorite smells in a long time, but one day Azalea said, "My favorite smell is Anthony when he dances with me." We both had danced with him that day and I thought he smelled like soap, but I didn't say so. Her feelings were personal. I was glad she confided in me.

"What do you think of Anthony?" Azalea asked me on one of our walks. I shrugged.

"I think he's cute," Azalea told me, "and strong."

She was right about that. I felt secure when he lifted me. "He's nice," I said, "but very quiet."

The street where our house was located ran between a church and an area with small shops. There were plenty of places to get takeout, but we rarely frequented them. One of the Libra Park families had been tasked with most of the cooking, so we generally all ate together. After supper was our favorite time for walking.

One time Azalea and I headed along our street, away from the shops, toward the church. Our plan was to walk along Washington to Cantine Park then back again. Along this track we generally passed a few joggers and dog walkers, but not so many people we were distracted from our gossip.

We started talking about Azalea's favorite subject, Anthony. The last few times she had been alone with him she had let him put his hands on her chest. To me this seemed a lot for a fourteen-year-old girl, but I'd never had a boyfriend. Azalea was excited to tell me what it felt like to hold him and how much they loved each other. I listened, nodded, but didn't know what to say.

The day was pretty, a warm spring day with light green leaves just starting to poke out on the branches of the trees that lined the streets. There was a gentle wind and a fresh, clean smell, like a baked pie just out of the oven.

We crossed Washington and turned left. We were

walking past the Methodist church when I heard the distinct sound of my mother's voice whispering to me. What I had heard years earlier in the sandcastle church was still clear in my memory and this was the same—the same tone and the same words, "sing and dance." I was certain.

I generally ignored the Methodist church each time I came this way, but this time I stopped and looked it over. "Did you hear that?" I asked Azalea.

"What?" She saw the direction I was looking and turned toward the church. "You mean the ringing?"

"Let's go look," I suggested.

She stepped back from me. "I'm not sure we should. It's private property."

"It's a church. Everybody's invited."

"That's on Sunday. Nobody's there now."

"Then nobody will see us."

Azalea was the big rebel when it came to her boyfriend, but now she was scared to walk with me to a church door. The main door was across a concrete terrace and up four steps. I headed that way. Azalea followed.

The smell was stronger now and sweeter. I recognized it as honeysuckle. I looked around and found a patch growing near a boxwood. Most people in our area tried to kill honeysuckle, but I liked the plant. It was strong and stubborn—qualities I admired. While I was looking I noticed the gentle sound was back. This time it was the ringing Azalea had heard rather than whispering. The sound was coming from close to the entrance to the church, so I kept walking. I moved up the steps to stand in front of the church door and looked around. I discovered a set of wind chimes hanging from a shepherd's hook placed near the boxwood. Honeysuckle had climbed partially up the hook, but the chimes still hung freely.

I stared, thinking of my mother as Azalea followed and stood next to me. She put her hand on my shoulder.

"What are you thinking?" Her voice was soft.

Azalea always knew when I had something on my mind.

There were four steps facing the wind chimes just like the steps facing the street. I felt suddenly tired, so I sat. "The sound reminds me of my mother."

Azalea got down on the steps and leaned against me. "Could the sound of the chimes remind you of how much she loved music?"

"It's more than that. She's speaking to me."

We sat there for a while staring at the wind chimes. They moved in the breeze every so often, just enough to keep my mother's voice coming through to me. They were so soft I was surprised we had heard the sound from where we had been walking.

After a minute or so, Azalea started to chant. She used a mantra Aunt Ellen had taught us in her meditation class—aham-prema. She had told us it meant "I am divine love." Azalea must have understood what was in my heart for her to choose that mantra. My mother was everything I thought of when I thought of love. She was reaching out to me through the soft sound of these gentle chimes.

The two of us chanted together, quietly, but with absolute sincerity. I lost all sense of the world until I felt someone touch me. Azalea and I turned at the same time.

A middle-aged man with a very round face was kneeling behind us, his hands on our shoulders. "I'm Reverend Adcock. I saw you two praying and wondered if I might help." He was bald, except for a rim of hair cropped very short and a beard that was also little more than stubble.

"We were meditating," Azalea told him.

He laughed ever so slightly. "I call that praying. Both words describe talking to God."

"I was talking to my mom," I said. I wanted him to understand this was about me and my love for Mom, not about his God.

"I see. Is she with God?"

I shrugged.

He stood up, struggling to rise as if he had weak knees. "I can let you into our sanctuary if you wish. It's a beautiful room and you can hardly hear the traffic when you are in there. Sometimes it helps to be in a quiet place when you want to reach out to someone you miss."

I shook my head.

"May we sit here a little longer?" Azalea asked. "Corinne likes the sound of your wind chimes."

"So do I," he told us. "That's why they're here." His eyes lit up. "You can stay as long as you want and come here as often as you wish." He pointed off to the side. "If you go to that entrance there's a doorbell. Ring it if you need anything at all."

The tone of his voice relaxed me. "Thank you," I said. He smiled and turned away.

We sat there for another five or ten minutes but the breeze had died down. The chimes were silent. Azalea went back to resting her head on my shoulder as we sat in silence, watching the chimes do nothing at all.

When I was certain Mom was done speaking I stood. She had drawn me to this church, then stopped without leaving a clear message. "Do you think Mom wanted me to meet Reverend Adcock?"

Azalea shook her head. "You said your mom wants you to sing and dance. He did not look like a dancer—a singer maybe, but not a dancer."

"Maybe they have a choir."

"How did you know it was her and not just something from the back of your head?"

"It wasn't my tone."

"And it was your mother's?"

"Yes, but that's not how I knew, not exactly. I felt a sense of calm all over when I heard the chimes, the way I do with some of my earliest memories of Mom singing to me and rocking me. And I could smell her hair. That's another memory from way back, the smell of Mom's hair."

"But isn't that what I was saying? Isn't memory just another word for something from the back of your head?"

"There's a difference. This was more real than a memory."

We decided to head back to the commune rather than walking on to Cantine Park. We'd had enough adventure for the day.

***

Azalea agreed to go back to the church with me for their Sunday morning worship service. We decided to wear our fanciest dresses, ones we'd bought for a school dance we went to. We'd found them with help from Azalea's mom. My dad was great at fixing things, but not very good at taking his daughter shopping. One of the advantages of living in a commune is if you need an adult to help you with something your own parent isn't good at, there are plenty of others available.

Mine was a light blue, half sleeve dress with a skirt that almost reached my knees. Azalea's dress looked a lot like mine, except it was black and had shorter sleeves and a longer skirt. She was self-conscious about her weight and thought black made her look thinner.

We asked Aunt Ellen if going to a church service was a good idea. I was worried she might believe it could interfere with our meditation training. She gave us a thumbs-up sign, leaned toward us and said, "There are thin places in our world—places where heaven and earth are closer. Maybe this church is one of those. In any case, anywhere you go to understand life and find your purpose is good for your soul."

Dad had once told me Aunt Ellen was always looking for answers, but back when he first met her she had a wild approach to the way she looked. "Now she's more philosophical," he had said. "I like her this way." I wasn't sure what a 'wild approach' was, but Azalea told me it had something to do with drugs. In any case, Aunt Ellen's words gave us the freedom we needed to see what went on within those church walls.

We walked to the church on Sunday morning and entered the sanctuary through the main entrance. There were a few people walking around, checking the sound system and making sure all the pews had hymnals and Bibles, but we were a little early so there weren't very many people sitting in the congregation. We walked down the center aisle and took a seat to the right.

The sanctuary was bright. The walls were painted off-white while the pews, the pulpit, the lectern, and the wall in front of the choir loft were all woodgrain stained dark. There was a black drape along the back wall with a table in front of it and a cross and open Bible on the table.

When others arrived, Azalea and I discovered we were overdressed. The only women other than us wearing skirts were as old as our parents. There were some younger people among the churchgoers, including two boys I knew from school: Doug Barre and Neil Lange. Azalea didn't know them, which surprised me. I thought she knew almost everyone.

The organist and the choir processed into the loft, then the choir sat and the organist began to play. While she played, more people entered until the sanctuary was about half full.

The minister entered after the music stopped. He greeted everyone in the congregation and gave a special nod to us. "I'm glad you took me up on my invitation to attend a service. It is wonderful to have you with us today."

The service had music and prayer and readings from the Bible. I expected all that. What surprised me was Reverend Adcock's sermon. His message was based on the encounter he'd had with Azalea and me earlier that week. "I looked out my window and saw two young women sitting on the church's front stoop. I watched and listened for a while as they chanted, sat silently, and chanted again. They repeated those steps a few times. I thought they were praying, so I went outside to invite them into our sanctuary. They politely turned me down, saying if I didn't mind they would like to stay where they were for a while longer. They called what they were doing meditating, but what I saw was two girls speaking to God and listening for his response. By my definition that is prayer and I believe we have much to learn from the way they were praying. We have a tendency to ask things of God—God grant me this or God grant me that. We also apologize to God—God forgive me for...blank. Then we fill in whatever we feel we've done wrong. What we don't do often enough is listen for God's answers."

Everyone in the congregation knew his words were about the two blonde girls sitting there. I felt as if the worshipers were staring at us, but when I glanced around the sanctuary I didn't see anyone looking our way. That's when I started to wonder if what I felt could be the spirit of my mom. Reverend Adcock thought we'd been talking to God, but we weren't. It was Mom we were reaching for. Maybe her spirit led Reverend Adcock to speak about our meditation. Maybe she was talking through him, saying she wanted us to return next Sunday and the Sunday after that.

After the service Azalea and I stood to leave, but an elderly woman in the pew in front of us turned to offer a welcome. While she was introducing herself I heard someone walking from the back of the church. I turned to see Neil Lange approaching. My head jerked back involuntarily, but I believe I caught my reaction before he noticed.

When the woman turned, Neil reached out his hand. "Corinne, I'm glad to see you here. Did you know Reverend Adcock planned to talk about you and your friend?"

I shook his hand. "We probably wouldn't have come if we knew." That wasn't true, but I said it anyway. "The conversation we had with him made us curious about what goes on inside this church. Since we live around the corner we decided to come to a Sunday service. This is Azalea, by the way. She lives with me."

"In the commune?"

"Yes, but how did you know that's where I live?"

"Everyone knows you live in the commune."

"We call our home Libra Park," Azalea told him.

My eyes went wide. "Everyone knows?" I asked Neil, ignoring Azalea's comment.

"Maybe not everyone. But I was curious. It's a different way of life from what most of us are used to."

When he said he was curious his eyes moved to my legs, causing me to feel a flutter in my belly. He took a quick breath and looked back at my eyes. I couldn't remember if Neil had been to the school dance where I'd worn this dress. This could have been the first time he saw me in it, or in any skirt. I always wore jeans to school.

I reached out and held his arm. "Anytime you want to know something about me just ask. I'm not a big fan of gossip."

"Sorry."

I let go of Neil when Reverend Adcock joined us. "Do you two know each other?" he asked.

"We go to the same school," I told him.

Neil nodded.

"I'm glad you came," the minister said to Azalea and me, "and I hope you come back. Maybe having a friend here will help."

On our walk back home Azalea said, "Neil is cute. Do you like him?"

"I don't know him very well."

"He sure looked like he wants to know you."

"You think so?"

"That line about him being curious about the commune wasn't true. I live there and he didn't even know who I was. I'm just saying if a boy knows where you live, he probably wants to get to know you better."

***

After dinner that night I asked Dad to come to my room. One of the problems with living in a commune is the lack of privacy in the common areas such as our living room. When I needed to talk to my dad alone we went to my bedroom or his.

"What's on your mind?" he asked after we shut the door and sat down. I was on my bed, leaning against the headboard. He pulled out my desk chair and sat there.

My mouth was dry. I didn't know what to say, so I started with Neil. "There is this boy."

"Oh dear." Dad fidgeted about, smoothing his pants legs. "I knew this time would come. Do you like him?"

"Actually, I know him from school, but we met again at the church service Azalea and I went to this morning. We spoke after the service and he seemed interested in me, at least that's what Azalea said."

"Okay." Dad took in a deep breath and rubbed the back of his neck. "I guess it's time for the talk."

I rolled my eyes. "We learn about sex in my health class so I know that stuff."

"That's good. Do you think about him in that way?"

"Dad?" I gasped. "We spoke one time and I hardly said anything at all!"

"I understand, but relationships can move faster than you expect. I just want to be sure you're careful and prepared."

"Prepared?"

"Yes. You're young and might not understand the feelings. I don't want you doing something you would regret later."

"That's not why I wanted to talk to you." I sighed. "Do you have any idea what Mom would say if she was here?"

I could see my question got to him by the way he frowned. "I can't tell you for sure, but I believe she would say the single most important decision you will make in your life is choosing the person or people you want to share it with. It should take you years to make that decision and there are lots of ways you can go. The most traditional is to find a boy you like and settle down to raise a family. Is that what you want? Because other choices are okay, too."

"I don't know what I want. That's the problem." My voice broke as I spoke.

Dad came to me. He sat on the bed and reached over and hugged me. "I know this is confusing, but it's not a reason to be upset."

"Earlier in the week I felt Mom's presence around that church." Dad released me, tilted his head and looked into my eyes. I kept on talking. "That's why Azalea and I went to the service, but when I sat in the church I couldn't feel her. There was too much going on. People were greeting me, the minister talked about Azalea and me in his sermon and then there was Neil talking to me after the service. I hardly had a chance to think about Mom much less speak to her." My voice trailed off.

Dad picked up my hand and held it. "I understand. On the day I met your mother she talked about how there's much more to life than what we can see and how important it is to keep searching. Whatever happens, I don't think you should stop reaching for her. If she's out there, and I believe she is, then she's doing everything she can to reach you."

"The minister said I could go there during the week and sit alone in the sanctuary."

"Did he? Would you mind if I go with you?"

"Oh Daddy, I would love that." That was the first

time I had called him Daddy in years.

***

It took Reverend Adcock a minute or two to come to the door after I rang the bell. He let us in and was as cordial as could be. Dad introduced himself and asked if we could sit in the sanctuary for a while.

"Of course you may. That's why we're here." He held the door as we entered.

The large window on the right side had stained glass bordered by clear panes. The bright sun shone through it so we didn't need to turn on the lights. There was a curved kneeler in front of the pulpit. I thought about going there, but decided instead to sit in a pew. Dad followed me down the aisle. He took a seat on the other side. We both needed to be alone to communicate with Mom.

The picture of Mom falling down the waterfall haunted me. I tried to push it out of my memory by reaching for an earlier image, one of her walking beside me or another of her pushing me on a swing. My effort didn't work and my eyes grew damp. I couldn't forget my part in her death. Still, I kept calling out for her, hoping my painful thoughts wouldn't keep her away.

I glanced over at my dad, wondering if he was having better luck than I was. It was hard to tell. He was very still, his head bowed in prayer. I couldn't tell if he was talking to Mom or to God.

I heard her voice saying, "I am with God," and I understood I was talking to them both. Since I had Mom's attention I spoke to her through my thoughts saying, "I don't know all the answers. Azalea's mom helps and Aunt Ellen helps and Dad helps, but I need to know what you think. I need to understand how you want me to lead my life."

I heard her say, "Sing and dance." The words were

as clear as if she was standing in front of me—shouting.

Gregory Hedden
Advice

My life was peaceful and I was happy. The days had been filled with routine projects that needed to be done around the commune. Corinne was a good girl. There were a few times I had to discipline her or console her or encourage her. What to do and say during those times was always clear to me. If she didn't do her homework, I limited her television time. If she was late to school, I made her go to bed earlier for a couple of days. Those were easy choices to make and things worked out well.

Suddenly I had complicated decisions to make and act on. Corinne was on the brink of a relationship. I didn't want her to get hurt but I had little experience to speak from. She was only fourteen but still—I didn't know what to tell her. After all, I was in love with a dead woman and my experience with Naomi had soured me on dating anyone new.

On top of that I was feeling mixed emotions about Corinne's experience in the church. Did I believe she had heard from her mother? I wanted to. Yet, if it was true, why hadn't Cyn contacted me? I had this strange mixture of joy that the soul of my wife had reached out to our daughter and jealousy that she hadn't reached out to me. Two days earlier I had been living a calm life. Now everything was hitting me at once.

Ellen was the only person I could think of who would understand my desire to contact Cyn but I couldn't ask her to help with my other problem. Her ideas about dating were unusual. She had two boyfriends who seemed to get along well. I didn't want Corinne to think that was normal. Fortunately, having a fourteen-year-old daughter who was just starting to date was something lots of other parents go through.

I thought Phyllis might be someone I could speak to. She was Azalea's mom. Like me she was a single parent of a teenage girl. We helped each other with tasks such as driving the girls to school or even babysitting when they were young. She also helped with some of my projects and I helped with the gardening. I considered her a friend, although I'd rarely had a conversation with her that went beyond platitudes. It would surprise her when I asked for real advice.

***

I had coffee with Phyllis in the kitchen of the commune house where she lived. "Corinne is in the early stages of her first relationship," I told her. Phyllis leaned across the table and patted my hand. Her sad smile told me she understood what I was feeling so I continued. "I don't know how to react. I don't even know if I *should* react." I shook my head and she nodded. "I told her she needed to be prepared but I didn't say anything specific."

"Prepared for what exactly?" Phyllis asked.

I rubbed my chin. "That's just it. I didn't tell her. The first thing I thought of was her getting pregnant—at fourteen. That scares the hell out of me. But first relationships can be hard in other ways. I don't want her to get hurt."

"You can't protect her from what this boy might do to her heart."

"I suppose not, but I could make it worse if I give her the wrong advice—or the right advice that she takes wrong."

Phyllis paused. "I've been thinking about this same thing. I tried to talk with Azalea. She's been dating a boy in the dance class named Anthony. They've been together for a while. I wanted to speak to her about birth control but she was embarrassed and cut me off. I didn't want to upset her so we never had the talk. Is that what happened to you and Corinne?"

"It sounds similar, except Corinne brought up the subject but didn't want my advice."

"Then what *did* she want?"

"To know what her mom would say."

Phyllis grabbed my arm. "Her mom?"

"Yes." I paused and frowned. "Or more accurately, her mom's soul."

She winced. "Oh my..." Her voice faded. "How long has your wife been gone?"

"Eight years, but that's not the point. Corinne is reaching out to her. That's why we went to the church."

Phyllis still had her hand on my arm. She began to gently massage me with her thumb. "I'm so sorry. That must be very hard on you."

"You don't understand," I told her, feeling my jaw grow tight. "I want her to reach out to Cyn."

"You do?" Her hand stopped moving. She blinked a few times.

I took her hand from my arm but held on to it. I wanted to tell Phyllis that people we've loved don't ever leave us, but I knew her story and didn't want to hurt her. Azalea's father left before Phyllis knew she was pregnant.

She looked down at our hands and said, "I hope someday someone loves me like that." She sighed and added, "I mean—a forever love."

I felt her hand moving again, drawing little circles on my skin. I pulled apart from her and said, "I guess we'll have to trust our daughters to do what's right. They're both smart, young women and they learn the basics in school."

Phyllis laughed. "Sex education," she said, more to herself than to me. She was right. The class was there to help not to replace me.

In the end Phyllis didn't have any advice that could

help me understand how to act as my teenage daughter started dating, but the conversation made me feel better. We decided to have coffee with each other again.

I had a few projects to do after Phyllis and I were done with our coffee. I had to repair a faucet, replace a pane of glass in a window in house seven and check on a porch light that had stopped working. It was eleven-thirty by the time I was done with those. I headed back to my house for lunch. I found Ellen in the kitchen making a toasted cheese sandwich for herself. She offered to make me one and I accepted. She poured me a cup of coffee. Although this would be my third cup that morning, I accepted it. I wanted the caffeine to help me think.

When we sat down to eat I brought up Corinne's comment that her mother had tried to contact her again, first through the wind chimes and then through a voice only Corinne could hear.

I fidgeted with the coffee cup. "I worry about the voices. Wind chimes are eerie. Most anyone could hear something strange in their sound. But voices? I wonder if something happened to Corinne that has caused her to think about her mother's death. It's been eight years since the accident and she has been doing well recently. I know she's interested in that boy she met at the Methodist church. Could that do it?"

"She might feel guilty if she thinks she's replacing her thoughts of her mother with thoughts of someone else. But I wouldn't discount the chance that Cyn is contacting her."

I frowned and tugged on my shirt collar.

"There are plenty of documented cases of people hearing the voices of loved ones who have passed. In most of those cases they say the voice is distinctly different from their own and sometimes there are other signs such as a feeling that someone is touching you."

"All she said was she heard Cyn's voice and was

sure it was her."

"Still..." Ellen scratched her cheek. "I know Corinne. You can believe her and I think you should."

"But why would Cyn contact her and not me?"

Ellen paused again before speaking softly. "There could be plenty of reasons. Contacting someone who has passed is difficult for the living. I imagine it is just as hard for Cyn and the others who are on the other side. Remember that and be careful not to let jealousy interfere with what Corinne is experiencing."

I considered her advice and decided to keep open to all possibilities.

I started having breakfast with Phyllis every Tuesday morning.

Corinne Hedden
A Confusing Dream

The Sunday after I heard Mom's voice, Azalea and I went back to the church. The night before Dad had asked if he could come with us, but I told him no. He was disappointed because he wanted to connect with Mom as I had.

"The church is too noisy on Sundays," I said, "We'll go back during the week and sit alone. Reverend Adcock is nice. He'll let us in again."

Dad reluctantly agreed, but I think he knew the real reason I didn't want him there. I wanted to talk to Neil without my dad hanging over my shoulder.

On the way to the church Azalea surprised me with more talk about her and Anthony. It seems they had tried a few other sex things. She wouldn't tell me what, so I said, "You be careful. You don't want a baby." I paused before adding, "Or an abortion."

Azalea stopped walking, crossed her arms and stared at me. "Do you think I'm stupid?"

I shook my head and we started walking again.

"Actually," she said, "our commune is not a bad place for someone our age to have a child, because everyone helps out."

She was right. Lizzy, a girl we knew who was about five years older than me, had a daughter a couple of years back. She was able to stay in school and planned to go to college. Still, she didn't go out much and always seemed tired.

Azalea grinned before saying, "I'd be a good mother."

I didn't want to hear that. "You're only fourteen," I told her, rolling my eyes.

"I'm just kidding, really. We know what *not* to do."

We? I hoped she wasn't depending on Anthony too much.

When we got to the church we went inside and took the same seats we'd been in the week before. A few people greeted us, but not as many as the last time. We were left with some extra time to sit quietly and stare at the cross on the altar. I listened for Mom, but didn't hear her.

Reverend Adcock's sermon was about freedom with an emphasis on "...the truth will set you free." It was a subject that didn't have much to do with my issues, but it made me think more about Azalea and Anthony. Were they being honest with themselves? It's hard to know when you're young and in love.

After the service, Neil approached me again. "Do you know Danny Corbin?"

"Not well, but I know who he is. Why?"

"He's throwing a party next Friday. I was wondering if you'd like to go with me. Danny's parents have a karaoke machine and he's allowed to use it, so they'll be singing and dancing. It should be fun."

Singing and dancing? My body went cold. *Could this be Mom's way of contacting me? If so, what is she saying?*

I started to answer but the words wouldn't come so I nodded.

"Great!"

I felt my body return to life and hoped I wasn't blushing. When I finally could speak I asked, "What should I wear?"

He smiled. "What you have on now would be great. We'll just be hanging out and having fun."

Azalea and I had dressed more casually this time. I was wearing jeans and a loose, purple top with a scoop neckline.

"I'll come by your house on Friday at seven, if

that's okay. We'll walk over together. It's about a half-mile. I'd rather do that than have my dad drive us."

"Fine with me. I love to walk."

***

I had a dream that night. Azalea and I went to Bobby's dance class and my mom was there. I started to run to hug her, but she turned away from me. She was busy talking with Bobby so I stepped back and waited with Azalea. *She didn't even wave.* I felt sick to my stomach.

Mom was dressed in a black leotard and tights with her feet left bare. Over her tights she wore the yellow, maxi skirt she'd worn on the day she died. I remembered it hanging on the tree branch halfway down the falls, waving over her body. I've hated yellow since that day.

Mom didn't look a day older. Her red hair was still thick and wavy. Her skin was unblemished and still the color of ivory.

"We're dancing with partners today," Bobby told us, taking my mom's hand and pulling her close.

Azalea ran straight to Anthony. Meanwhile, I looked around the room expecting to have to dance with one of the other girls. I was surprised to discover they weren't in the room and Neil had shown up unexpectedly. I went to him and stood by his side. He put his arm around my shoulder.

"Watch this," Bobby told us. "I want you to copy what we do." He put his hands on Mom's waist.

Mom started dancing to show us what we would have to do. She went up on pointe and I was horrified. She wasn't supposed to do that with bare feet. She could hurt herself. Then I noticed her toes weren't touching the ground. She was fluttering her feet about six inches above the floor. Could Bobby be holding her up with such ease? I didn't see how.

Bobby twirled her then let go. Mom glided from

him, spun until her skirt ballooned into a pedestal of yellow ripples. Then she floated back to Bobby's arms and he lowered her to the dance floor.

"Next," Bobby told us. I looked down, hoping he wouldn't call on Neil and me. He didn't because Azalea and Anthony stepped forward.

Somehow Azalea had changed her clothes. When we arrived at the class we were both wearing leotards and tights with jeans over them. We both had on black tights, but my leotard was blue and hers was pink. We shed our jeans in the class so we could dance. Now, as Azalea was about to dance with Anthony, the leotard she had on was black and she was wearing my mom's yellow skirt.

I'm not sure exactly when I figured out I was dreaming, but by this time I had. So I wasn't surprised by the fact that Mom's skirt fit Azalea perfectly despite two facts: Mom was much taller and Azalea was pregnant, very pregnant.

Aunt Ellen had taught me about lucid dreams. I knew what to do even though this was my first experience with one. I told myself Azalea was not pregnant and watched as her belly shrunk. This was fun, but I was not going to waste the dream revising my image of Azalea. I looked at Mom who was standing beside Bobby dressed only in her black leotard and tights, no longer wearing the skirt that years ago had messed with her balance and thrown her down the waterfall.

I concentrated as she walked toward me. "I love you, Corinne," she said. It was nice to hear, but it was my dream—the words weren't hers.

"Would you watch us, please," I asked my mom. Then I turned to Neil and said, "Dance with me."

I had always thought dancing was as close to a perfect dream as I could have, but dancing in my lucid dream was beyond anything I had ever imagined. It was heaven. Neil lifted me with his right hand on my back. I was bent backward, facing the ceiling with my eyes closed, my legs down on one side of him and my arms and back down on the other. I felt as if I was resting on God's hand.

Prokofiev's Romeo and Juliet filled my heart as I drifted above Neil. While Mom had fluttered above the floor I was flying as high as the ceiling, floating when the music was gentle, soaring when it was furious. I glanced down. Neil was watching, giving all his attention to me like a fox watching a duck that had taken to the air.

My mom stood and shouted, "Stop!" Neil reached to catch me as I fell, but he was slow and dropped me. I woke up.

***

Plenty of the people in our commune claimed the ability to interpret dreams, but everyone agreed Aunt Ellen was best. I went to her and arranged a session. We held it in her room because that's where she had a little table set up for everything from candle meditations to seances. Uncle Sean and Bobby were told to stay out of the room while we were there. They would go share a pizza and a few beers while they waited.

After I told her my dream, Aunt Ellen slid her chair close to the table and leaned toward me. "How well do you know Neil?"

"Not well. He's nice. He's good-looking and he seems to like me. I guess that's the most important thing isn't it?"

"What *you* feel is more important," Aunt Ellen argued. "But you can't make a decision without spending time with Neil. He might be perfect for you. You just don't know it yet."

I sighed. "We're not here to talk about Neil. I need help with my dream. I think my mom was trying to say something to me and I don't know what it is!" I didn't mean to sound angry but I was getting frustrated.

"I'm sorry." Aunt Ellen took in a deep breath and let it out slowly. "Your mom's spirit told you to sing and dance when you were a child playing in that sandbox, right?"

"Yes. And she told me the same thing just this past week when Dad and I were sitting alone in the church." I lifted my hands, palms up. "But I don't understand. Is she saying I should concentrate on a professional career in singing and dancing? My dad says Bobby could introduce me to the right people."

I smiled, then switched back to explaining what was bothering me. "Neil has invited me to a karaoke party where there will be singing and dancing. Maybe Mom's actually saying I should go with him. How am I supposed to know?"

"You're only fourteen. You don't have to make life-altering decisions. Go to the party. See if it's fun. If it doesn't leave you feeling fulfilled try performing in something more challenging than one of Uncle Sean's productions. Bobby can help you with that."

"But maybe I shouldn't be making my own decisions. Maybe Mom has my life mapped out for me. What I really want to know is—what is Mom trying to tell me?"

We were quiet for a short time until Aunt Ellen broke the silence. "There's something odd about Azalea in your dream."

My chest grew tight when Aunt Ellen mentioned Azalea's name. "What about her?"

"Why was she pregnant in your dream?"

I didn't want to answer that question. Azalea had told me in confidence how she and Anthony were experimenting. Telling anyone would be a betrayal of her trust. Also, in our commune people talked—a lot. Anything I told Aunt Ellen about Azalea and Anthony's relationship would surely get back to Azalea's mom. "Maybe it was a warning," I said. "Maybe Mom was trying to warn me about what could happen if I let Neil get too close."

Aunt Ellen nodded. "That certainly sounds like her. Your mom never regretted having you, but her pregnancy did change her life." She paused. "There's another possibility," she added, frowning slightly. "She could be pushing you to lead the life *she* wanted. Cyn was kind, but ambitious."

The life I cut short.

We were quiet again, the two of us scratching our temples and rubbing our chins. Finally, Aunt Ellen said. "Your dream isn't as clear as it could be—except in one aspect."

"What's that?"

"Neil dropped you at the end. That *is* important."

We'd taken our discussion as far as it could go and I wasn't any closer to understanding the meaning of my dream. "What should I do next?"

"We need to talk to your mom's spirit."

"We?"

"We need to include your dad."

Aunt Ellen was always living along the edges of the paths traveled by others. We were in a commune so we were already far off-center, but Aunt Ellen was extreme. I had heard from my dad how she had once been into drugs but now her focus was spiritual.

"Should we try now?" I asked.

"Her spirit is not here. You felt her at the church, right?"

I nodded.

"Then that's where we need to go."

Aunt Ellen leaned toward me and focused on my eyes. "I want you to go back to the minister and tell him we need to use his sanctuary. Her spirit is there. Given a chance, I believe we can reach her."

What she said made sense. I decided to speak with

Reverend Adcock after church on Sunday, but Friday came before Sunday so the party Neil had invited me to was what I was thinking about. The way Neil had dropped me in my dream was important, yet I still wanted to go. I wanted a chance to get to know him.

Corinne Hedden
Karaoke

The afternoon of the party I tried on some outfits. I decided on a pair of tight jeans, dark blue ones, and a black tank top with a light denim jacket over it. I tried on a few other combinations but settled on the blue jean look. I went to Azalea's house to get her opinion. She said I looked great and had me stand with my back to her full-length mirror while holding a handheld one so I could see the outfit from the back. The jeans fit like they were painted on.

Azalea stood with her hands on her hips and looked me up and down. "You will be the best-dressed girl there, but can you dance?"

I hadn't thought about that. I could hardly bend over.

She went to her closet and pulled out a hanger with a denim skirt on it. "Try this. It's tight on me. I think it will fit you."

The skirt was the same color as the jeans I was already taking off. When I got it on, the fit was perfect. I did the same mirror routine to look at my back. It wasn't as tight as the jeans had been, which was a good thing I suppose. I bent forward and squatted a couple of times. I could move in this. I decided to wear tights with the outfit, black ones. That would make it perfect.

Neil showed up at seven, as he had said he would. It was late August so the nights had started to get a little cooler and I was as comfortable as I could be. We walked in silence until we were in front of the house next door to mine. It was one of the commune homes and had a flower garden in front, like all the Libra Park buildings. This one had daylilies, hostas, and roses.

Neil was walking with his hands in his pockets and looking down. He seemed as nervous as I was. He glanced at the house we were passing, pulled his hands out of his pockets and said, "These gardens always make the houses you people share so beautiful."

I can't say I was happy he'd referred to us as "you people," but at least he was trying to reach out to me. I think he wanted me to see he knew something about Libra Park. Yet it wasn't what I wanted to talk about. I asked him what he liked to do for fun.

"I love music."

I grinned. "I love music too. That's something we have in common."

I worried I might have come on too strong, but he seemed pleased. "Do you play an instrument?"

"Piano. We have a Yamaha in the music house. It's a spinet, but a nice one. We also have an electric piano."

"The music house?"

"It's the third house down on the other side of the street." I pointed to it. "I take lessons from Miss Rizzo, a woman who lives there. Everyone in Libra Park has responsibilities and helping us with music is one of hers. That's how we work here. My dad is good at fixing things, so anytime there's a problem with the plumbing or the electric he's the one they call. Everyone has a role here."

"So what do you do?"

"I'm like all teenagers, I guess. I go to school and try to figure out what I want to do with my life. Isn't that what you do?"

"I suppose so."

I moved closer to him and brushed his arm with mine. He smiled and took my hand. That felt nice.

"How about you?" I asked. "Do you play an instrument?"

"I play sax and clarinet, but guitar is the instrument

I'm best at. I spend a lot of time sitting in my room trying to imitate my favorite musicians. I've never had formal lessons."

"I'd like to listen to you sometime."

"Sure. I have some friends I play with."

"You're in a group?"

"Sort of, but nothing formal. We're thinking of practicing a little harder and trying to play somewhere, maybe a battle of the bands. We've got a drummer, a bass player and me."

By this time we had turned right on Main Street and were approaching Mynderse Street. We turned right again. Danny Corbin's house was just down the block. We could hear the karaoke music.

"Maybe someday I'll play for you and you can play for me," Neil suggested. "I could bring my guitar to where you have the piano."

"I'd like that."

When we got to the house we saw a lot of cars parked along the street. We walked in through the front door which was wide open. Somebody was singing *Cara Mia* by Jay and the Americans and he was absolutely horrible. There's this long note in the song and the longer he held it the more off-key he went. He was so bad I was worried the entire evening might be painful, but some of the other singers were good enough. Neil asked me if I'd like to dance.

"Sure."

This wasn't like dancing in the studio, but it was fun. Neil wasn't self-assured so I didn't try to do anything fancy. At least not until he suggested we try karaoke.

"What kind of songs do they have on that machine?" I asked.

"There's a huge variety. They have a book that lists everything."

I leafed through the book and found they had what I

was looking for, a Broadway category.

"I don't think the other kids will appreciate those songs," Neil warned me. "Most everybody sings the current hits and some oldies. Show tunes? That's just not their thing, but I like them."

"Then I'll sing for you."

I started out with *Sunrise Sunset* from *Fiddler*. There was some applause, but only from a few of the kids there. I had to take it up a bit. Next I sang *Don't Cry for Me Argentina* from *Evita*. There were moments in that song where I could shine. Uncle Sean and Bobby both thought it was one of my best pieces. Yet, once again, the students at the party gave me a so-so reaction. Neil was right. I needed a song they were familiar with. I picked *Send in the Clowns* from *A Little Night Music*. It had been a hit by Judy Collins. Everyone recognized the music and went wild with my version. I could tell Neil was proud he was with me.

After my three songs no one else wanted to sing. Danny put on a Madonna CD to keep the music going. When *Crazy for You* began Neil took my hand and pulled me to where we could dance again. This time he put his arms around my waist and I put my arms around his shoulders. We were slow dancing to Madonna which seemed odd but this was a song that worked for us. He pulled me close. I could feel his legs moving against mine and I liked the feeling. Neil was not great at fast dancing but this was amazing.

Later, when we started walking back to my home Neil asked, "How did you learn to sing so well? You hit every note perfectly."

"I've been singing since I was a kid. I take classes."

"At Libra Park?"

"Of course."

"It must be nice, living in a commune."

We'd been holding hands, but when he said that, I put my arm around him and we walked as close as possible.

Some kids I knew were suspicious of commune life, but others were envious. I was glad Neil was in the latter group.

Neil stopped walking. He tilted his head slightly and bit his lip before asking, "Would you consider something?"

"Consider what?" My heart was pounding. I thought he might be asking me out on another date.

"You know how I said the guys I play guitar with are thinking of getting more serious with our music once we're in high school?"

"Yes?" Was he asking me to come listen to them?

"We need a lead singer and you would be perfect."

That is what he wants?

My mind was racing with possibilities, but I couldn't commit because I wasn't sure what Mom would say. This was singing and Mom told me to sing. But this wasn't dancing and she told me to do that as well. I needed to talk to her before I could give him an answer. I wasn't sure Reverend Adcock would let us use the sanctuary and, even if he did, I wasn't sure Aunt Ellen could reach Mom's spirit.

"Perfect?" I asked.

"You would be the best."

"Could I play piano, too?" I stammered, hoping my question would show I was interested even though I hadn't given him an answer.

"I don't see why not. If you play even half as well as you sing you would add so much to our group."

"Let me think about it."

He seemed disappointed, but he nodded as we started walking again.

It felt strange walking in the dark since I rarely went outside this late. But I was with Neil and I felt safe. After we turned the corner onto Main Street there were lights from the shops even though, except for a couple of restaurants, they were all closed.

We didn't always talk as we walked. I didn't feel a need to fill the silence and I guess he didn't either, which was nice. When we reached my house I wasn't ready to go inside. I suggested we sit on the stoop for a while. At that time of night there were few cars, so sitting there was peaceful. I leaned my head on his shoulder and he put his arm around me.

"Are you going to church on Sunday?" he asked.

"I need to speak to Reverend Adcock so I will definitely be there."

"That's nice. I'd like to sit with you if that's okay."

"I'd like that, but just so you know I'll be with my dad, Aunt Ellen, and probably Azalea as well."

"That's fine, but save me a spot next to you."

We stood and moved to the front door. I thought about asking him to come in for a while. It was past midnight so nobody would be in the living room. But I was tired and I'm sure he was as well. He looked a little awkward and I felt my knees wobbling as we stood facing each other. I decided to make the first move. "Would you like to kiss me?" I surprised myself by being so forward but it worked. He smiled, then we kissed and it was wonderful. My head spun and my whole body grew warm. This was my first real kiss. My kisses with Azalea didn't count. Those were just practice—to be sure I was ready for this moment.

When we separated his eyes were wide and glowing.

"See you Sunday," he said as he stepped away. At the bottom of my stoop he turned to wave. I was still staring.

***

Neil held my hand during the Sunday service and afterward, when everyone in the congregation stood to leave, he reached for me again. I loved this. It wasn't as if Neil was my boyfriend but he was letting everyone in this public place know there was an *us*.

We walked with my dad, Azalea, and Aunt Ellen to the exit where we had a chance to speak with Reverend Adcock. "We would like to meet with you during the week," Aunt Ellen told him. "We want to hold a private prayer session dedicated to Corinne's mother. She died nine years ago. Would you be willing to let us use your sanctuary? Corinne says she feels her presence in your church."

I noticed she didn't use the word seance. Reverend Adcock smiled and agreed.

We returned to the church on Tuesday afternoon. Since school was not yet in session, I didn't have a conflict and Azalea could join us. Reverend Adcock led us to the sanctuary. Once there Aunt Ellen suggested we sit on the floor in the area between the pews and the pulpit. Reverend Adcock was surprised but didn't object even though he had more trouble than the rest of us getting down into a sitting position.

We closed our eyes and the reverend opened with a prayer. "God, Corinne misses her mom a great deal. Please reach out to us. We all need comfort. Amen."

Aunt Ellen took over when he was done. She spoke directly to Mom. "Cyn, please speak to us. Corinne has heard you say 'sing and dance,' but she is having trouble understanding what you mean. She is fourteen, the age where she will start making her own choices in life. I have tried to help as have the other mothers in our group, but nothing is the same as her own mother's advice. Some of the choices she makes now will affect the rest of her life. Send your words to help Corinne understand."

After Aunt Ellen's plea we were silent, sitting in our little circle with our eyes closed. I felt Mom in the room around us and once again I heard her voice. At first her words were scrambled and distorted, but they gradually became clear. She was saying "sing and dance," the same words she had said before. I called out to her in my mind. I wanted to know what she meant. I could sing with Neil or I could try for something bigger. Bobby could connect me with people who could help me start my career, but they were in New York. If I turned Neil down and met with them, I would have to drop out of school and be tutored like some of the other girls in our commune. I would see much less of Neil. Yet if I went with Neil and ignored the other opportunities I would be relegating my career to something small. Is that what I wanted?

My mind went to Neil as I thought about the choice I needed to make. I was thinking of the feeling I had when Neil kissed me. I didn't love him, but I did love the way he made me feel. Could I give that up? When I remembered his arms around me, my mom's voice faded. I lost touch with her.

When our prayer session was finished I asked the others if they had heard her voice. Everyone, including my dad and Azalea, told me they had felt and heard nothing. I was the only one Mom contacted. Without any more advice than the three words she had offered me, I had to make up my own mind. That's when I decided I would join Neil's band.

Gregory Hedden
The Breakfast Hour

The meals Phyllis cooked were nice when compared to the milk and cereal I generally ate for breakfast and her strong coffee was always welcome. We would talk at the table when no one else was there. If we couldn't have privacy in the kitchen we would move to her bedroom. This wasn't unusual in Libra Park. Everyone moved to their bedrooms for private conversations. Even our daughters met in their rooms when they wanted to talk without us hearing.

Phyllis always dressed casually for our morning discussions, usually in jeans and a blouse or a sweater. She wore her jeans tight but liked loose-fitting tops, probably because she was a little heavy. She always appeared attractive but never sexy. Her outfits didn't show much cleavage, any perfume she wore was subtle and her makeup was limited to eyeliner and lipstick. Her appearance was never at all seductive, which is one reason she managed to surprise me one day when we were alone in her room.

"I want to speak to you about something, Gregory." Her head was tilted slightly. "We've gotten to know each other very well and I love that. You're one of the best friends I've ever had." Her right hand was near her ear. She was twisting and untwisting a lock of her short, light brown hair. "The fact that we have daughters who are best friends makes us even closer."

"Of course." I nodded in agreement.

She took in a breath and let it out. "I'm a little nervous about saying this. I don't want to mess up this friendship but I need to say something."

That worried me but I didn't let it show.

"Okay. I'll just come out and say it." She paused again. "Since we first started meeting for coffee and talking over our problems I've been feeling a little less lonely. No. A lot less lonely." She smiled. "That's wonderful but it's also brought out other feelings."

"Feelings?"

"Yes. It's like smelling coffee brewing and never getting a cup to sip on. Do you understand what I'm saying?"

"Not exactly."

"I'm saying our friendship has reminded me of how much we are missing and that makes me sad."

"Do you want me to stop talking to you? Because I don't want that."

"I'm not suggesting that at all. I just...well...let me come out and say it. I want you to spend the night with me."

My eyes went wide. "You mean sleep with you?" It was a stupid question. How could she have been any clearer? But she had knocked me for a loop. Even though Phyllis was five years older than me, she looked younger and very attractive.

She nodded and looked down. Her arms were folded across her chest.

"You know we can't do that," I told her. "Azalea's room is right beside yours and if we went to my house, Corinne's room is beside mine. They would know what we were doing and that would send the absolute wrong message. Remember, the reason we started meeting was to discuss how to approach our daughters as they start to feel their own sexual needs."

"I know," she said, looking up at me again. "But couldn't we work something out?"

"I've always been upfront about how I feel." I stepped to her and took her hands in mine. "I care about you but I'm still in love with Cyn. It would be unfair to you."

"Unfair to me?" She tried to step back but I didn't let go of her hands. "You know what? This feels unfair to me." Now she pulled on my hands bringing me so close to her we were almost touching. "Talk is what I wanted to begin with but right now I want more."

She brought her lips up to mine and kissed me. It had been so long since I'd tasted a woman's lips I couldn't help myself. I kissed her back and as soon as I did that we fell on the bed and started pulling at each other's clothes.

I felt awkward when the sex was over and I believe she felt the same way. We were lying on our backs, staring at the ceiling, not saying anything. After a minute or so I rolled to my side and got up off the bed to search for my clothing. She did the same thing, still without either of us speaking.

When she had pulled her panties on and was getting ready to put her bra on, she stopped, lowered her hands and took a step toward me. Her eyes grew wider and she said, "That was nice. Thank you."

I felt myself blushing as I replied, "Sure." I took in a breath and added, "Yes. I...uh...thought it was nice, too." I watched her put on her bra and finished putting my own clothes on.

When we were dressed Phyllis straightened the bed, sat down and started to talk about an issue she'd had with Azalea. I sat beside her, keeping enough distance that our legs didn't touch. I can't remember what Azalea's problem was.

***

After that morning, sex became part of our routine—at least once a week, more often twice. It was different sex than what I had experienced with Cyn. Phyllis wasn't built like Cyn had been. She was shorter and much thicker. Also we had to be quiet which included our breathing and any noise the bed might make. But the oddest difference was the way she never forgot to thank me, the way she might thank a waiter who had just refilled her coffee. For a while I tried to reply but I could never think of the right words to say. After a few months I fell back on a small smile and a quick nod. I told myself this was fine as long as we both knew we were having sex, not making love.

Corinne Hedden
Chante et Danse

I convinced Neil and his friends to call our group *Chante et Danse*. I suggested *Sing and Dance* first, but the guys did not like the English version so we switched to French. Even though we were all just freshmen, we soon became the most popular band in school. We were that good. It seemed everyone in school wanted to be my friend.

Neil picked the music we played and everyone in the group said they loved his choices. Yet my favorite moments were when Neil and I would sing two-part harmony, soft songs I chose. He would sing the melody down an octave while I played his electric keyboard and sang harmony. I would look in his eyes as we hit the perfect chords and resolved smoothly. It was a form of intimacy I appreciated more than the other intimacies we shared. I guess that was good because we didn't get as much time alone as I wanted. We were always practicing or performing with the group and after a while that got a little old.

In the middle of our junior year, at a gig for Mary Ann Lindgren's birthday party, my life changed radically. *Chante et Danse* was in top form. My notes were spot on and my range was the best it had been since the cold weather began. The guys were playing well, even though they were all sneaking drinks. If I could judge the evening by our music, it would rank as a wonderful night. However, halfway through that party I discovered Neil playing something other than guitar.

We were taking a break and I went upstairs to use the Lindgren's bathroom. I'd never been in Mary Ann's house and somehow opened the wrong door. I was standing in her bedroom where I found her and Neil on her bed. His shirt was on the floor and hers was pushed up to her armpits.

Mary Ann was the first to see me because Neil was on top of her, his face buried between her small boobs. She raised her eyebrows and appeared to suppress a laugh which quickly turned to a grin. Neil rolled over. When he saw me he gasped and tried to cover his naked chest with his arms.

Mary Ann lay there through all of this, not even bothering to pull her bra and shirt back down. I suppose some of her reaction was because I was a popular girl and she'd just put me in my place. Yet there was another reason, probably more important to her. She knew Neil was now free to be with her whenever she wanted him. Just like in that dream I'd had two years earlier, he'd dropped me.

What surprised me was how little this scene bothered me. In fact I almost laughed as I watched him reach for his shirt and scramble to put it on. I finished the gig that evening, even led everyone in a verse of Happy Birthday as Mary Ann stood in the center, turning and nodding to all her friends.

Azalea and Anthony were at the party. His dad picked them up and I rode home with them. Azalea must have known something was wrong since I wasn't riding with Neil but I didn't tell her what had happened until the next day.

In the morning I went to her house and knocked on her bedroom door.

"I'm sleeping," she said, sounding groggy. It was Saturday, about eight in the morning.

"It's me," I said loudly enough she could hear me through the door. "I need to talk to you."

Azalea opened the door and let me in. Her hair looked like a squirrel had been living in it. She was wearing her plaid pajamas: blue, purple, and white. Her feet were bare.

I walked past her and sat on her bed. Azalea turned toward me and tilted her head slightly. "Have you been crying?"

"No. Well—maybe."

"What did Neil do last night?"

"I caught him with his hands and mouth all over Mary Ann." I rolled my eyes. "Giving her a birthday present, I guess."

Azalea shook her head and muttered, "I thought something like that had happened."

"You don't understand. I don't care about him."

"Your eyes are red and there are dark circles under them. I think you care—a lot."

"Not really. Mary Ann can have him."

"Then why were you crying? You can talk to me. I'm your best friend."

"I know you are but you're not my mom and somehow this thing with Neil has made me miss her more than ever. That's what's happening. I don't care if I lose Neil but losing him reminded me of losing Mom. This thing at Mary Ann's party—it brought the pain back."

Azalea stroked my hair, then sat on the bed and hugged me. I started to sob again and we both fell back on her mattress, our arms around each other, my face buried in the curve of her neck. She rocked me gently as if I was an infant and I felt like one.

"We need to do something," she whispered to me when I started to get control of my emotions. She was stroking my hair again. "Maybe we should jump Mary Ann when she isn't expecting us. We could scratch her face and tear her clothes. That would show her not to mess with you."

I wiggled away from Azalea and sat up. "You don't seem to believe me. This has nothing to do with Mary Ann or with Neil. It's about Mom. I killed her and all the emotions, the guilt and the sorrow, all that is coming back."

Azalea stood and I noticed she had been crying, too. "Then we need to come up with something else, something to get you closer to your mom. You know she's out there. You know she's watching. She's spoken to you. You have to find a way to talk back and listen better."

I shook my head. "Easier said than done."

"Maybe there's another place where you can be closer to her? Maybe there's another way of meditating you haven't tried yet."

"I doubt that. Aunt Ellen's looked into every possible scenario."

"Maybe we can go to some other religious group, some cult that knows how to speak to the dead? You need to find your mother's soul. Think what that would mean, not only to you but to everyone who has lost someone they love."

She was right but we didn't come up with any answers that morning. Still, Azalea got me thinking.

***

There was nothing that would keep me connected to Neil after the Mary Ann incident, no baby on the way or history of him holding my hand while I suffered through an abortion. I'd lost my virginity to him in the fall when I wasn't on the pill. We were lucky that one time and didn't go so far again. I told him I would, but apparently Neil didn't want to wait and Mary Ann was available.

I know this seems backward because I no longer had someone to be with, but after I lost Neil I asked my dad to contact our doctor so I could get birth control. I didn't want to ever be in that situation again. She was easy to talk to, especially since Dad was on board with me taking the pill.

Chante et Danse was scheduled to play at the school for the winter formal a week later. I agreed to sing there as well, although I refused to speak with Neil about anything other than our music. I told Bobby what had happened and he brought his agent, Donna Taylor, to hear me. She was impressed and now, at sixteen I was again faced with the same choice—school or career. This time, however, my relationship with Neil pushed me toward the opposite decision.

The choice wasn't easy. I was enjoying my high school years. If I signed on with Donna Taylor I would be giving up my conventional life. I wasn't sure that was a good thing. It had been a long time since I'd reached out to my mom, but I needed her now.

I thought more about Azalea's suggestion to "find my mother's soul." I decided to go to North Carolina where she was buried. Perhaps I could find her spirit near her gravesite.

Corinne Hedden
The Number Seven

I scheduled my trip for winter break right after Christmas. At first, Dad said he wouldn't go with me. He didn't get along with Mom's parents. They still blamed him for Mom's death even though it had been more than nine years since the accident and I had explained repeatedly how I was the one responsible for what had happened.

"Can I drive alone?" I asked him. I already knew he wouldn't let me go such a distance without an adult in the car but I was hoping my question would help change his mind. I thought he might suggest I fly down and have Grandpa pick me up at the airport. That's what I normally did on my annual Easter visits. So before he could bring up that option I said, "Or you can come and we can stay at a hotel."

"They won't like that." He was talking about Grandpa and Grandma, of course.

"If we get Aunt Ellen and Azalea to go with us we'll have too many people to stay at their house. That could be our excuse." My grandparents loved Aunt Ellen. They'd known her since she and Mom were best friends in grade school. Apparently, they didn't know her drug history, but that was old news now.

Dad gave a hint of a smile which quickly vanished when he said, "They'll want you with them."

"Well, they can't have me without you."

He nodded and the smile returned.

"What about Azalea's mom?" I asked. They seemed to get along well. They ate together every morning and spent lots of time together, probably complaining about me and Azalea.

"I don't think she'll come. She hates driving long distances." He had a small smirk I didn't understand. I thought I'd ask her anyway.

Aunt Ellen and Azalea both agreed to go but Dad was right about Azalea's mom. She said Azalea could go but she didn't want to.

Aunt Ellen suggested we take some detours on the trip down. "The number seven is a powerful spiritual number. Seven days in a week, seven days in the creation story, seven candles on a menorah, seven days between the phases of the moon. The list goes on and on." We were talking in her room. Aunt Ellen was lying on her bed looking at a seven-pointed star she had painted on her ceiling. I was sitting next to her. At this moment she sat up so she could look into my eyes. "If we want to have the best chance of reaching your Mom's spirit, we should prepare on the way down. We should stop at the seven most important places in her life and death. If we do that we will be reaching out to her and readying ourselves for the visit to her gravesite."

"What places are you suggesting?"

"The first place is here. She found peace and joy in our commune, especially in the theater. We should start our trip on the stage where she performed so often."

"And then?"

"The next place we should stop is Buttermilk Falls—where she died."

"B-Buttermilk Falls," I repeated, stammering a bit. It would be my first time there since the accident. I was scared of the memories but maybe it would help me get past some of my anxiety over that day. I clenched my jaw and agreed.

After that Aunt Ellen wanted to go to the original Woodstock site in Bethel, the place where Mom and Dad met. That sounded fun and, like Buttermilk Falls, was close by. When we were done there she wanted to take us a little out of our way. She intended to drive to New Brunswick, New Jersey where she wanted us to stand outside the hospital where Mom gave birth to me.

"If possible we will step inside the lobby," she told me. "But going there is what is important even if we stay outside."

That made four places. We had three more to go and it turned out they were all in Greensboro.

"I want to go to the building on the UNCG campus where your dad and I saw your mom dance. It was the first time he saw her perform and that was as important to her as it was to him. After that, I want us to visit the hospital where your mother was born for the same reason we will visit the place where you were born."

"Then we go to her gravesite?"

"Her gravesite is important but it doesn't count as one of the seven. We should check in with your grandparents before we go there. Their house is the home where your mother grew up and the last place on my list. The first stops will take time, so we should plan to stay over in Maryland. I'll leave it up to you to make a reservation."

I found an inexpensive motel and reserved a room. I called Grandma to tell her our plans. She offered to put us up but backed off when I said there would be four of us, as I thought she would. She didn't complain about Dad even once. However, Grandma's reaction to bringing Azalea with us was strange.

"Azalea? What kind of a name is that?" I could tell by her tone she was prejudging my friend. She didn't like the fact I lived in what she called a hippie commune.

"It's her name," I told Grandma. "I never thought about it being different. It's just her."

"It's a plant."

"So are daisies and roses, yet those make nice names."

I told Azalea what she'd said, but Azalea didn't seem to care. "As long as they don't give me a hard time when we're there I'll be happy. I'm looking forward to this trip and to seeing what happens along the way, especially at your mom's gravesite."

When it was time to go the four of us met at the theater house where we had a small ceremony. Aunt Ellen and Dad both reminisced about shows Mom had been in and I mentioned my favorite of the songs I'd heard her sing, her rendition of *Memories* from Cats. I didn't mention the irony in the fact that all I had left of my mom were memories.

We didn't go back to the house down the street where Dad and I lived, but we talked about it. It was where Mom had spent the last five years of her life and where their marriage ceremony took place.

"That is important," Ellen told me with a gleam in her eye, "but I count Libra Park as one stop. This is where your mom's life with you and your dad took the best direction for her. It's where she managed to be an actress, a singer, and a mom with help from both of you. All of that was rolled into her love for this place."

Those recollections weren't what I would call prayers. Yet they did help us get into the right mood for our pilgrimage. When we were done inside we left the theater and crammed into the Libra Park Ford Escort. It was licensed to Aunt Ellen, but belonged to all of us in the commune. Aunt Ellen was driving with Dad riding shotgun, while Azalea and I sat in the back seat.

When we were in the car, heading up to Buttermilk Falls, I quietly said the prayers I had not spoken during the short ceremony. I prayed this journey would bring me closer to my mother, would help me understand how she felt about her life and would teach me what she wanted me to do with mine.

"That was beautiful," Dad told me.

I hadn't realized he'd heard me. I was glad I had not given voice to my most heartfelt prayer, the one I'd been keeping to myself for years—that Mom could forgive me.

The trip to Buttermilk Falls Park took less than a half-hour. After we left our car we had to walk a short path. I wondered if the park rangers might have put a fence around the area after the events that led to my mom's death. They hadn't. They must have wanted to keep the setting rustic.

We all stood at the top of the falls looking over the scene. None of us smiled and Dad was crying. The sculptured rocks and the foam from the running water in the creek were like a lace ribbon running through someone's hair. An angel perhaps? Or a devil? I thought it was wrong that the waterfall looked magnificent. This place had caused the worst event in my life. How could it deserve such beauty?

I wondered about Hell. I wondered if there might be something enticing about that dark place, something there to draw unsuspecting innocents to an eternity of torture. After all, isn't that what this place had done to me? I didn't step out on the stones because I wanted to prove how brave I was. I wandered out there because I wanted to see an awesome sight.

I moved away from the others, off to the right where I could attempt to speak to Mom's spirit with some privacy. "Why isn't life fair?" I asked into the empty air. If there was any way I could go back to that day I would throw myself down the falls rather than let her climb out after me. She was the one with so much potential. I was just a snot-nosed kid going where I wasn't supposed to go.

I thought about jumping to end my pain. But I didn't believe Mom wanted me to follow her that way. She wanted to guide me in the way I lived my life. I took a couple of deep breaths and stared at the flowing water when someone grabbed my hand from behind. It was

Azalea. Why hadn't she realized I wanted to be alone?

She moved closer and strengthened her grip. "I had a miscarriage," she told me in a whisper.

"What?" I couldn't believe I'd heard her words right. *Isn't that something that happens to older women?*

"Remember when I had a stomach ache and had to skip a couple of days of school. Well—it wasn't just a stomach ache. There were also backaches and bleeding down there." She pointed her nose toward her lower body. "The doctor told me I'd had one. I hadn't even known I was pregnant. She asked if I was on the pill and I wasn't. Anthony and I had always been careful. It was enough for years, but not that time."

"I'm so sorry."

"I wasn't faced with the abortion question because my body did it on its own, but I don't know how to feel about this. I saw you standing here thinking about your mom and I wasn't going to say anything. I know this may be the worst time for me to tell you. But I could see your emotions and I just couldn't help myself."

She was talking fast, starting to ramble. I pulled my hand out of her grip and held it up to stop her. "How far along were you?"

"It was the first month. The doctor said a lot of women have miscarriages in the first month. I didn't know that. All those things they teach us in sex ed, but there's still so much I don't know. I mean, what about the baby's soul? Did it have one?"

"I don't see how. That early it couldn't have been much more than a fertilized egg." I couldn't think of what else to say to console her, so I gave her another hug. That was the best I could do.

"I know you lost a person," Azalea said, speaking softly as we continued to hug, "and what I lost was something else. Yet I still have this empty feeling inside."

This was the other part of the dream I'd had where

Neil dropped me. Azalea had been pregnant in my dream and became pregnant in real life. I was holding her, rocking back and forth and crying. Still, I couldn't help but feel a tiny spark of joy because Azalea's confession meant my dream was real. Mom had contacted me with something other than a soft voice saying, "sing and dance." What's more—the things she told me did not happen until years after my dream.

I released Azalea, took her hand again and walked back with her to where Dad and Aunt Ellen were still standing. I thought it was time to go and hoped they would agree. They did.

After we left Buttermilk State Park and were heading south on 96, Azalea scooted close to me and leaned her head on my shoulder. I put my arm around her and leaned my chin against her head. I loved the smell of her hair.

Dad turned around in his seat to look at us. He had a dazed look when he saw us snuggled up against each other. "Are you two tired already?"

"No," Azalea said without opening her eyes. "We're just getting comfortable."

She might have been comfortable, but I had a bit of a crick in my neck. I squirmed a bit until she sat up. "Sorry," I told her, pulling my arm from behind her. "My neck hurts." She sat up and hung her head so I squeezed her leg lightly. "You're the best friend anyone could have." She smiled at that. My dad was facing the front now saying something to Aunt Ellen. I whispered to Azalea, "Thank you for confiding in me."

Corinne Hedden
Woodstock and A Birthplace Revisited

As we approached the festival site we passed a ranch-style house with a well-manicured lawn. "That was where we set up camp," Aunt Ellen told us. "The house is new. Back then it was an undeveloped lot with a few trees and lots of vines and shrubs."

Dad pulled the car over and stared. "I met your mother at the concert site but we walked back here. It was our first day together." I knew the story, of course. He'd told it to me countless times. "Yes," he repeated softly, "the first day we met."

The way his voice changed when he repeated his words made me wonder if something more than just talking went on at that place. When I counted the months between the date of the festival and the day I was born, I knew I couldn't have been conceived on this land. Yet, something special happened here.

We parked our car by where Aunt Ellen and Dad thought the food stand and art show had been. "Everything looks different than what I remember," Aunt Ellen told us. Dad agreed.

We walked down through the audience area toward where the stage had been. The grass was cut close. I assumed most days they had quite a few people strolling the grounds and had to keep it low. After that we walked over to the pond where they had gone swimming.

"Should we take a dip?" Aunt Ellen asked.

Dad looked at me and pursed his lips. "Are you talking about skinny dipping?"

"Why not?" Aunt Ellen replied.

Dad paused and shook his head. He was still looking at me. That's a problem with dads. Lots of things that are fine for the rest of the world are out of bounds for their daughters.

"Remember, we're not here for you to relive a wild moment. We're here to bring back memories of Cyn. She did not go in the water."

"I'll go in," Azalea volunteered.

"If you do," my dad told her, "your mom will hear about it."

"She won't care."

"No," Aunt Ellen told Azalea. "Gregory is right. This is supposed to be about Cyn, not about what *I* did that day. We should meditate over the pond the way she did, not bathe in it the way I did. We should concentrate on what was important to her. She loved us and we loved her. Now we need to focus all our attention on her. She is trying to speak to you, Corinne, and we all need to help you hear."

We formed a semicircle on a grassy area with a slight slope. The open side of our half circle faced the pond. We held hands, closed our eyes and all said silent prayers. When our prayers were over and we had all opened our eyes, we followed Aunt Ellen's lead and sat on the ground, keeping our semicircle intact.

Aunt Ellen crossed her chest with her arms, her open palms touching her shoulders. We closed our eyes again. "We are at Woodstock by the pond where you and Gregory watched me swim. We're remembering that day and hoping your soul can remember it as well."

"We know you are out there," Dad said. "We know your soul is eternal but we miss you. We need to hear from you. We need to know what you feel. We need to understand your opinion of what we've done with our lives since you left us."

That's when I spoke. "I miss you so much, Mom. I'm so sorry for what I did to you."

"No!" Dad shouted. "You were a child. It was my fault. I shouldn't have let you wander off alone."

Aunt Ellen interrupted us both. "We shouldn't focus on the accident. We are at the festival site now, not Buttermilk Falls. This is where Cyn and Gregory met. This is where their story began."

"It's not just their story," Azalea said. "It's all our stories." She spoke a little louder as she turned her voice to Mom. "We know you are with the ones who went before you. Tell us about them. And tell us about the souls that never had a chance." I opened my eyes and stared at her. I understood how much she'd lost. I didn't believe the embryo could have had a soul, yet she still loved it in her own way. I guess I said all that with my expression because Azalea's chin trembled as she stared at the pond.

Aunt Ellen and Dad must not have seen her sad look because they still had their eyes closed. Aunt Ellen started to chant, "Om."

I closed my eyes again but only after I had moved close enough to Azalea to take her hand.

When Aunt Ellen was done chanting Azalea began speaking, softly at first. "Corinne is my sister in every way except blood." She raised her voice. "You were a second mother to me, Aunt Cyn. Uncle Gregory was the father I never had. I reach out to you now asking for help. Corinne is suffering without your guidance. Like me, she is just sixteen years old and facing some hard choices. She needs your guidance. You've offered hints but they aren't enough. Speak to her, please, not just for her sake but for all of us."

"That was beautiful," Aunt Ellen told Azalea as we walked back to the car. "I'm sure she heard your words. Hopefully, she will follow them."

The next leg of our pilgrimage was going to be longer than the first two, a couple of hours at least. Dad drove us east on NY-17B, a two-lane highway but one where the traffic seemed to move well. We passed White Lake on our left as Aunt Ellen began to explain the importance of our next destination. "The place where any woman gives birth is always significant in her life. You are Cyn's only child, which makes it even more meaningful. However, you are the person who came into being in that place, so it is vital for you and your life. We are asking your mother for advice concerning your life. Remember that."

"I do," I told her.

"Good." Aunt Ellen twisted in her seat to look at me. I was still in the back with Azalea. "Do you know the time of day you were born?"

I shook my head.

"Do you?" she asked my dad.

"No."

"That's unfortunate, but there is still a lot of information we can draw from the day." She reached into a plastic grocery bag she had kept by her feet and pulled out a paperback book. "You were born on July 30th 1970." She started to read. "The sun was in Leo, the moon was in Cancer, Mercury was in Leo, Venus in Virgo, Mars in Leo, Jupiter in Libra, Saturn in Taurus, Uranus in Libra, Neptune in Scorpio, Pluto in Virgo, North Node in Pisces, Lilith in Leo, and Chiron in Aries."

Aunt Ellen's spiritual beliefs never ceased to amaze me. She seemed to accept all religions and combine them into one large mass centered around two basic beliefs—that God is real and our souls are eternal.

"Your north node is the most important of these. It represents your destiny. In your case you have a tendency to worry too much and to suffer from feelings of guilt."

It didn't surprise me how well Aunt Ellen had me pegged. She knew I felt responsible for my mother's death. What was amazing was she wasn't just saying this stuff. She was reading it out of a book.

"The only way to deal with these problems is through belief in a higher power which is why you need to continue to attend church."

"I've been doing that," I told her, feeling my stomach tighten.

"True," Aunt Ellen said, sitting up as straight as she could while twisted around in the passenger seat. "It's just that you've gone through a lot with Neil. Don't let what happened change how you feel about church. If Neil makes you uncomfortable at the one near Libra Park, find another. What's important is you keep attending somewhere and you keep God in your mind and heart."

"I'll do that," I promised.

"The sun in Leo gives you many strong qualities. You're determined and ambitious. You should also have a strong sense of self-assurance. I see that aspect of your nature in many things you do, but when it comes to your mother your self-assurance fades. You will have to deal with that for your mother's soul to have a chance to reach you. The moon in Cancer has made you sensitive and highly creative. Those are also tools you can use to help her find you." Aunt Ellen formed her hands into a steeple and brought them to her lips. "Keep all this in your mind when you are standing in front of Robert Wood Johnson hospital, the place where you were born."

Everything Aunt Ellen said made me nervous as we approached New Brunswick. I thought if I didn't keep my mind straight I might block Mom from reaching me. I told myself over and over to relax and stop worrying, but I had trouble making that happen. I prayed, but my nervousness continued.

Maybe Dad realized what I was going through, I'm not sure, but when we finally reached New Brunswick he suggested we go by his old apartment before heading to the hospital. I bowed my head and thanked God for Dad's suggestion. Perhaps the extra time would help stop my self-doubt.

Dad's old apartment complex reminded me of our

commune houses because they were townhouses in long rows that were close to the street. There weren't any flower gardens between the narrow porches and the road here, but there was one long strip of grass. It was impossible to tell how large the units were, since we couldn't see how far back they reached, but they all had upstairs and downstairs windows.

"Even though we moved to Libra Park before I was a year old," I said, speaking more to myself than the others, "this place was where I had my beginning. That has to be important."

Aunt Ellen pushed her hair back. "It's not where you took your first breath. We're going there next. And remember, you moved to Libra Park before you were a year old."

I suppose she was right, but seeing this place, where Mom, Dad, and I had lived as a family, sent chills up my spine. Maybe it was because I'd lost Mom at such a young age, but I saw this apartment as something special.

"We can't go in," Aunt Ellen announced. "We might as well move on to the hospital."

I could tell Dad was reluctant, but he agreed.

Robert Wood Johnson hospital was an enormous building. I'm not sure how much of it had been added in the last sixteen years, but even half of the place was huge. I felt a sense of wonder with the realization that I was standing in front of the building where Mom had pushed me into this world. I wondered if this place had been a start for my life or just a stop on a long journey. I hoped for the latter because if I've always been and always will be around, then so will Mom.

We went inside, entered through revolving doors and found ourselves in a large lobby. The room was decorated in modern ways I was sure had changed since the day I was born. There were red and brown walls and art carefully hung behind the receptionist desks.

Aunt Ellen approached a woman sitting at one of the desks and asked for the maternity ward. I was a little nervous as I wondered what she was planning. I could picture Aunt Ellen walking into the hospital room of some woman who had just given birth and explaining we were visiting my old room. I couldn't think of anything more intrusive than that. But fortunately she looked over the maternity ward then led us around the halls and back to the lobby where we found seats and each said a prayer.

Azalea gave thanks that she was allowed to be part of this trip. I think she was really thanking Aunt Ellen but she said the prayer was to God. Dad said his silently and Aunt Ellen tried once again to speak to Mom saying, "Corinne's birth was the most important part of your life, Cyn. We are here celebrating that event and reaching out to you once more."

When it was my turn I said, "I love you, Mom. I always have, even when my body was part of your body. Believe me when I say what I feel for you is always and forever." I looked at Aunt Ellen after I said those words. She was breathing heavily and had her hand over her heart.

Corinne Hedden
Secrets Revealed

We ate lunch in the hospital cafeteria before we walked to our car and headed south. The plan was to stay in a Days Inn I had located in Maryland. It would take us about four hours to get there. When we arrived we planned to check-in, have dinner, and settle into our rooms. We'd reserved two, one for Azalea and Aunt Ellen and one for Dad and me. Azalea suggested she and I take one of the two rooms, but Dad nixed that. "Two sixteen-year-old girls alone in a room?" He grinned. "I don't think so. You two would never get to sleep."

Under normal circumstances I might have been offended by his comment. Azalea and I were more mature than he thought we were, but this time I was okay with him splitting us up. Truth is, I was worried about him spending a night alone with Aunt Ellen. She already had two boyfriends, Bobby and Uncle Sean. I could see her wanting a third, especially if the man was Dad. They'd always been close, even when Mom was alive.

As we drove to Maryland the conversation began with reminiscences of Mom, but gradually turned to things like performing. Dad knew all about the group I'd been in with Neil and had even attended a few of our concerts. Aunt Ellen, however, had no idea how successful we'd been.

"That's over now," I told her.

"I wouldn't be so sure. You could put together another group if you wanted to. I'm sure you could find a drummer and nowadays everyone plays the guitar."

She was right and if I couldn't find another group, I could do a solo act. I was pretty good with folk music. The fact that I had options was what made my decision so hard. Should I stay in school or sign on with Bobby's agent, Donna Taylor? Either way I would be singing and maybe dancing a bit as well. Hopefully, this trip would help me get more from Mom than those three words, *Sing and Dance*. I needed her advice.

We ate dinner at the restaurant in the Days Inn. We all had spaghetti with sides of green beans. Pasta was the best selection we could find on the menu for Aunt Ellen and Dad who were vegetarians. I joined them since I was trying to give up meat. My time with Neil hadn't helped me. He loved cheeseburgers. Azalea ordered meatballs with her spaghetti. She had no desire to switch to a plant-based diet, not even when she was traveling with us.

When we were done eating we went to the room where Azalea and Aunt Ellen were going to stay. The room my dad and I were sharing was not next to this one, but both were on ground level.

"We shouldn't talk about the pilgrimage or what might happen at the gravesite," Aunt Ellen suggested. "Instead we should use this time to get our minds clear and to have fun." I went to turn on the TV, but Aunt Ellen asked me to keep it off. "Television is so passive. Let's play cards. A game of Hearts will give us a chance to talk about other things in our lives."

We all knew how to play Hearts. There was a game going on almost every evening in the common room of the house beside Azalea's home. I played once in a while and Azalea loved the game.

The motel room wasn't huge but we managed to set up a place to play. There was a table between the beds. We slid it out a few feet, removing the lamp and clock radio and placing them on the floor. We climbed into positions around the table with Azalea and Aunt Ellen sitting on one of the beds and Dad and I on the other bed facing them.

While Aunt Ellen dealt the cards she suggested we

tell stories. "Would you start, Gregory? Tell us something we don't know about you."

"All right," Dad told her. "Here's something I did that was a little crazy." My stomach rolled a bit when he said that but I didn't ask him to stop. I didn't think either Aunt Ellen or Azalea would judge me by something crazy my dad said.

"I had this friend, Tim, in high school. He was one of the guys who went with me to the Woodstock festival. When we were sophomores we knew this pretty girl we both had a crush on." He turned to me to say, "This was years before I met your mother." He turned back to talk to all of us. "We were young and immature so our way of showing we liked someone was to play a prank. When her birthday came around, Tim and I bought a jockstrap, gift-wrapped it and gave it to her in biology class. We thought that was a suitable place. Anyway, she had no idea what it was, pulled it out of the box and held it up for the class to see. She shrugged and looked confused until the girl sitting next to her leaned over and told her to put it down. Our friend was a good sport and took the prank well."

Just like the girl from Dad's past, Azalea had no idea what a jockstrap was. His effort to explain was funnier than the story. Soon we were all giggling. He was laughing so hard he foolishly played the king of spades on Aunt Ellen's ten. I had the queen so I dropped it, he took the trick and with it the thirteen points I thought I'd be stuck with. His laughter stopped after he saw my move so I started telling my story.

"Neil and I went to lots of parties when we were a couple. Our group was playing at most of them. When we finally went to one where we weren't the entertainment we found it was boring. It didn't help that the only music there was on a radio station turned up too loud.

"Six of us decided to drive over to the lighthouse on the river. It was late and the trail through the nature preserve would be closed but we chose to go anyway. We knew we could get past the gate and Charles, the boy with the car, had a flashlight so we would be okay."

I turned to Dad. "I wouldn't have gone if I wasn't with Neil." He nodded but didn't smile.

I continued my story. "Charles' car was small. Only four could fit in the seats. Charles told us the trunk had room for two if the ones locked in it didn't mind cuddling close. It was decided Neil and I, being a couple for so long, were the ones to ride back there and I didn't argue. We were locked in and stayed there until we felt Charles park the car. Then we heard him get out and close his door."

If Azalea was the only one I was talking to I might have mentioned that the short time between the door closing and the trunk opening was important because we had to get our clothes straight. I didn't want either Dad or Aunt Ellen to hear that part.

"Charles let us out. There was a locked gate in front of the Saugerties Lighthouse Trail. That didn't stop us. We jumped the fence and started walking through the woods. We were okay until Neil and I started to hang back and lost sight of Charles and his flashlight."

Here's the next part I censored. We intentionally lost the others after Neil slipped his hand down my jeans. Once I was sure we were alone, I put both my hands down his.

"Neil kissed me and I kissed him back. When we opened our eyes we couldn't see much. The night sky was partially covered in clouds and the moon wasn't out. It wasn't as dark as I had suspected it would be but it was still hard to move without bumping into things. We decided we could lose the path if we tried to catch the others so Neil and I sat on the ground and waited for them to return. When they did, we all went to the gate, climbed back over the fence and headed to our homes. It was a wild night but a good memory."

Aunt Ellen and Azalea both thought my story was cute but Dad's expression was less than pleased.

Azalea suggested she would go next. "I'll tell you something I've only told one other person." She looked at me. "That person is Corinne, but this is still a secret from the rest of you."

"Go on," Aunt Ellen told her, speaking gently.

"I'm sixteen years old and I've been pregnant."

Dad gasped, but Aunt Ellen didn't even flinch. "Like in Corinne's dream?" she asked.

Azalea raised one eyebrow. "Dream?"

I sighed. "You were in the dream I had, the one where Neil dropped me. You were pregnant. Only you weren't just a month along. You were big. You had to be close to giving birth."

"A difference doesn't mean the dream didn't come true," Aunt Ellen interrupted. "Your mother was telling you Azalea would be pregnant. She knew it before it happened."

"Can we get back to my story?" Azalea asked.

Aunt Ellen apologized to Azalea and said, "Go on."

"Okay." She took in a breath. "I had a miscarriage. I didn't have to make a decision about keeping the baby or not keeping the baby. That was made for me by my body or by God or whatever you want to say. Still, I can't help feeling a sense of loss. There was someone inside of me and then there wasn't. This happened in the first month so I guess you can't say it was a person, but still..." Azalea ran her hand over her forehead before continuing. "That's why I am so desperate for Corinne to hear her mom's voice. If Aunt Cyn is out there the soul that would have been my baby is there, too."

Aunt Ellen's eyes were wet. She clenched her jaw before saying, "To go through what you've gone through at such a young age has to be painful. You're handling it with a maturity well beyond your years. Whatever happens, if you ever need anyone to talk with you please come to me. I'm sure Corinne and Gregory feel the same."

It was Aunt Ellen's turn to tell something about her past. She had a very serious look on her face and started to open up about her life. "I suppose you've heard I experimented with drugs when I was younger. I don't know how much you have been told but it was worse than just that. I sold them. I was just having a good time, enjoying my youth. I sold to friends and friends of friends. I wasn't looking for new people to bring into the drug culture. That never even crossed my mind.

"I did have *some* ethics. I decided I would sell to college kids since they were doing all these things anyway. I did not sell to high school students. That was my rule and I stuck by it, for the most part. Then this young kid, a junior in high school, approached me at the restaurant where I was working. He started talking about buying stuff from me where others could hear him. I needed my job so I told him to go away but he kept coming back.

"He would meet me as I was leaving work and try to talk about it there. That wasn't much better than in the restaurant because other people were leaving at the same time. He was so persistent.

"I don't know why he didn't go to somebody else. Greensboro was not drug central by any means but I wasn't the only person selling. This boy was a shy kid. I guess he had heard about me and didn't know where else to turn.

"I finally said I would do it. He tried LSD and liked it. Apparently, he lost his inhibitions while he was high and impressed some girl he was interested in. She liked him as well, at least that's what he told me. He also told me he couldn't talk to her when he didn't have the drug so he needed more. He kept needing more and he kept coming to me.

"I wonder if I might have stopped, if I hadn't been making so much money off him. I feel guilty about that."

She breathed in and out before continuing.

"The boy killed himself. The paper said it was over a girl, probably the one he'd only been able to talk to when he was high. There was an autopsy and there were no signs of alcohol or drugs in his system."

"No signs of drugs?" Dad asked. I was surprised he didn't already know the story. I guess Aunt Ellen had kept this secret to herself all these years.

"That's right," she told him. "I try to think about that often, to ease some of my guilt. But they didn't find his body until a couple of days after he died. Maybe they just tested his blood rather than a more thorough test. LSD only lasts about twelve hours in your blood. Also, people sometimes lie to save the reputation of the dead. If that was the case, I'm guilty as hell."

"If he was a junior he was our age." I glanced at Azalea and back at Aunt Ellen. "That makes him old enough to make his own decisions."

"He was still a teenager," Aunt Ellen told me. "Old enough to make lots of *wrong* decisions." She tried to laugh, but her smile seemed more like a grimace. "One good thing came out of this. I gave up drugs, both selling and using and began looking for God. I didn't go to church. Instead I went to the library in Greensboro. I started researching religions: Christianity, Judaism, Islam, Buddhism, Hinduism, Taoism, Astrology, Wicca, Faerie Faith, Sikhism, Spiritism, and Native American religions. You name it, I looked into it. When I finally moved out of the library and tried to find examples of those religions, I found Uncle Sean and Libra Park. That's not much compensation for a life lost, but it is something good."

We all agreed. Her work with us at Libra Park had been wonderful and now she was helping me connect with Mom's soul.

Corinne Hedden
Greensboro and The Gravesite

I slept well that night. Dad snored, but it was a light snore and it comforted me rather than keeping me awake.

The next morning Dad and I knocked on Aunt Ellen and Azalea's door and the four of us walked to The Waffle House where we had breakfast. When we'd finished eating and drinking way too much coffee, we went back to our motel, checked out of our rooms and headed south. We stopped for lunch on the way down I-81, but arrived in Greensboro after four. We checked in at our motel which was another Days Inn, then we went over to the UNCG campus. We left our car at the Walker Avenue deck and headed over to the building where my dad had first seen my mom perform. It was an old brick building but the classic design fit well with the other buildings around it.

The doors were locked. We had to wait until a careless student walked out, allowing us to grab the door before it shut. No-one stopped us after we were inside so we went up one floor and poked our heads into an empty classroom, the one where Mom's performance had taken place years ago.

Aunt Ellen and Dad seem to be tickled to be back at the spot where they had sat together to watch Mom. This place meant a lot to me because it was where my father found my mother after his crazy search for her. But other than that it wasn't special. It seemed much like any ordinary classroom. I certainly didn't get the same magical feeling I had at our other stops.

We stepped into the room and looked around. A couple of college-age women followed us in but Aunt Ellen asked us to say quiet prayers anyway. When I opened my eyes I saw the two women were standing very still and staring at us as if they'd caught us stealing. One of them had grabbed the other's arm but they didn't say anything. We left the room, went back to our car and on to our next stop, Moses Cone Hospital.

I was impressed with the building where my mom had been born. I asked Aunt Ellen if she was going to look up the horoscope for my mother's birthday as she had for mine at Robert Wood Johnson hospital in New Jersey. She shook her head. "She's in another life now, another world. Her horoscope should still affect her, but in ways I don't comprehend. It would confuse us more than it would help us. What we're going to do here is enter the building, find the chapel and send prayers to God and to your mom's spirit."

We followed her instructions with each of us saying our prayers silently. My prayer was simple. "Reach out to me Mom. I need you." I said those two sentences over and over again and finished by saying. "Please God, help her do that."

***

The next stop was Grandma and Grandpa's house, where we were going to have our dinner. Everything started out well. Grandpa was cordial to all of us, including my dad. He offered us drinks, red wine for Dad and Aunt Ellen, cokes for Azalea and me. We chatted about the trip down and Aunt Ellen discussed how she had missed Greensboro. "There were good memories here," she told my grandparents, "especially in this house. I loved you both when we were kids."

"And we loved you," Grandma said.

After a while I asked Grandma if I could go up to the guest room where I stayed on my annual visits.

"Of course you can," she said, smiling at me. "When you're here it is your room."

I knew it was not only a guest room. It had also

been my mom's room when she was a young girl. "Can Aunt Ellen come with me?" I asked.

Grandma and Grandpa nodded at the same time so we went upstairs and closed the door.

As soon as we were alone Aunt Ellen instructed me to think of a short but powerful thought to send toward Mom's spirit. She said I should not share this thought with her or anyone else. "It is important to keep your meditation personal and internal. Close your eyes and imagine this place in the darkness of night." That wouldn't be hard for me to do since I had slept there many times over the years but before I followed her instructions I went to the window.

I pictured myself younger, four years old, the age I was a year before Mom died. I remembered being in this room back then, pulling a chair up to this window so I could climb onto the window sill and look out at the backyard. I could see the neighbors' homes tucked behind the trees of what seemed like a magical forest. Was I seeing what was out there now or what had been there when I was so much younger?

I pulled a strand of my hair in front of my eyes and saw it was more red than blonde and I realized I was no longer myself. I was my mother at four, looking out the same window I had looked out. The image of me as my mother seemed so real I turned from the window and faced the mirror. My mother's image wasn't in the glass. I was sixteen again, standing in the room with Aunt Ellen.

Was this another way of Mom reaching out? I wasn't sure. I looked at Aunt Ellen. She gave no indication that she'd seen the transformation I'd experienced. Since I was alone in this I decided not to speak about it. Perhaps it had all been in my imagination.

"Are you alright?" Aunt Ellen asked.

"I'm trying to think of the best thoughts to send to Mom.

She smiled. "Just think the thoughts that are in your

heart."

"I will."

"Do not speak again, until we rejoin the others."

I thought of something from my childhood and put the other experience out of my mind. Most experts in childhood memories will tell you anything you remember preceding your third year will be fabricated. Our sense of self is unformed at that age so eventually we experience something called infantile amnesia. Yet I must be different. I can still remember my mom holding me when I was two. I had fallen and scuffed my knee. I was crying. Mom picked me up. She took me to a soft chair where she gently rocked me. I intended to focus on the intimacy of being held by my mother.

I talked to myself without uttering a sound out loud. "I feel your arms, Mom. I hear your heart beating. I smell your hair and your skin. I sense something coming from you that can only be described as love." Those are the words I silently formed inside my head. I paused for a second and I swear I could feel her response. I could feel that same sensation of adoration I had felt when I was so young. I combined this love I had felt for her with the earlier experience I had of *being* her and decided this last of the seven stops was the best of all.

I opened my eyes when I heard Aunt Ellen open the door. We headed downstairs in silence. We had used our time well but the rest of our visit with my grandparents was a total disaster. Grandpa abided by the agreement to treat my dad well but Grandma wasn't speaking with him. As we rejoined the group I heard her bringing up Azalea's name.

"Is it a hippie name?" she asked.

Azalea blinked a couple of times and said, "I'm not really sure where it comes from, but it's my name and I like it."

That conversation was a good indication of how the

rest of the visit was about to go. When I had visited my grandparents previously, it had always been just the three of us. They were fun and cheerful, a little pushy about their church, but that was okay. As Aunt Ellen would say, it's important to believe in something. Today was different. I'd never seen Grandma so ill-mannered. I knew she blamed Dad for Mom's death and would never get over that, but she'd agreed to be nice. The way she was acting wasn't even close to that.

Then came dinner. Grandma had made a baked chicken along with green beans and mashed potatoes. She had put bacon bits in both the beans and the potatoes. Grandma knew Dad was a vegetarian and had probably planned this for his sake. What she didn't know was that Aunt Ellen had also given up meat. They both took bread on their plates and skipped everything else. When I saw what they'd done I wondered how I should react. At first, I thought I'd pass on the bread because that was all they had to eat but instead I decided to join them.

Azalea was the only one in our group who took anything else. She put potatoes and green beans on her plate, skipped the chicken, then started to pick out the bacon bits and push them to the side. She wasn't a vegetarian. She was just helping us make our point. I loved her for that.

Grandma was horrified. I thought she was going to scream. Grandpa stopped her before she could by putting a hand on her shoulder. "This isn't working out. Let's go to the K&W."

There were plenty of choices at the cafeteria. The only one of us who didn't eat was Grandma. She was still steaming. She hardly spoke a word at the table. After dinner we headed to the cemetery. It was summer so there was plenty of light even though it was after seven.

Grandpa led us to Mom's grave. I thought Aunt Ellen would have prepared a ceremony and I was a bit worried about the way my grandparents would react. Instead we all said silent prayers once again. Mine was the same one I'd said at the hospital. "Reach out to me Mom. I need you." Aunt Ellen also prayed. When she was done she pulled a sandwich bag out of her pocket, dug a little dirt with her fingers and stored the soil in the bag. She then slipped the bag back into her jeans. If there had been a lot of dirt, the bag wouldn't have fit in her pocket. Those were the tightest jeans I'd ever seen on anyone older than thirty. No one said anything about what she did, but I looked around and noticed everyone watching her.

We had our car at the cemetery because we had driven separately. When our prayers were done we said our goodbyes.

"You're still going to visit us at Easter, right?" my grandma asked as I walked her and Grandpa to their car. I had hoped this would do for my annual visit but I could see hope in her eyes and in Grandpa's as well.

"I'm a vegetarian now," I told her. "Will you honor my choice?"

"I'm sorry. I didn't know."

"You knew about Dad."

"I did, but I was thinking of you—not him."

There was the problem. I didn't make an issue of it, since I knew it wouldn't do any good. I told her I'd be back, hugged them both and they left. After they drove off, we headed to the Days Inn.

When we arrived at the motel, Aunt Ellen said, "We need to gather in Gregory and Corinne's room for a ceremony. This is the final step."

We went straight to our room. When we were inside, she looked at my dad. "Pick up your toothbrush and whatever else you need. You will sleep in our room tonight. Corinne must be alone."

He looked at me. I shrugged and he stepped to the sink to get his stuff. He slept in his underwear, so he didn't need to bring pajamas or anything other than his toiletries and what he was wearing. Both rooms had two double beds in them, which meant Aunt Ellen would be sharing hers with either Dad or Azalea. I suspected Dad would be her choice.

"Would you show us what you sleep in?" she asked me.

Unlike my dad I did change when I went to bed. I hadn't unpacked and had to find it in my suitcase. It was a nightgown, light blue with short sleeves. The gown reached my knees. It was thin and cool but reasonably modest.

"You need to put it on," she told me.

I stepped into the tiny bathroom which consisted of a tub/shower and a toilet. The sink was in the main room. I took off my clothes, folded them and slipped the nightgown on. I considered leaving my underwear on, but that wasn't my normal routine and Aunt Ellen had asked me to wear what I always wore. I wasn't embarrassed since Dad was the only man with us. He saw me in my nightgown every night when he kissed me goodnight.

As soon as I opened the door to the main room I was hit with the smell of incense. Aunt Ellen had lit three sticks and placed them on the bureau. I knew we were about to hold a ceremony, hopefully one powerful enough to help me contact Mom.

"Sit in this chair," Aunt Ellen instructed, pointing at the straight-backed chair that had been at the writing-table. She had moved it by the door, the only place in the room that had some space. I did as I was told. Someone had pulled the curtains shut. No one could look in from outside.

Aunt Ellen had one of the disposable cups in her hand. "This is mud made of dirt from your mother's gravesite."

That explains the sandwich bag.

"I need to make a mark." She dipped one finger in the cup and rubbed it on my forehead. The previous year I had attended Ash Wednesday services at the church with Neil. This felt very similar.

Dad approached me with another cup. "Here. Drink this."

I shook my head. "If I drink that much water right before I go to bed, I'll have to get up to pee."

"Exactly, and getting up will help you remember your dreams."

I guzzled it down. He took the empty cup from me and tossed it in a wastepaper basket.

Aunt Ellen had brought a cassette player which she placed on the bureau with the burning incense. She turned it on. I heard flutes, drums, bells, and cymbals. The sound caught my attention even though the volume was set low.

Azalea, Dad, and Aunt Ellen formed a single line. They circled me three times then stood staring at me. Aunt Ellen whispered, "This is one of Taoism's eight great spiritual mantras." And she began to chant in a low, soft voice.

The Cloud Seal
of the Great Void.

Existing since the
beginning of a
great kalpa.

Suddenly near and
suddenly distant.

Perchance sinking or
perhaps floating.

Moving back and
forth through the
Five Directions.

I'd never heard Aunt Ellen's voice like that. It was so low she sounded more like a man than the woman I knew. The chant ended with this:

Supporting those
drowning in toil
and Earthly dust.

Assistance will come
for those imprisoned
in desire.

Bringing ascension
into the Immortal
Realms.

We waited in silence for about ten seconds before my friends began to move. Azalea stepped to my bed and pulled back the covers. Dad and Aunt Ellen helped me to my feet and led me to the bed. They helped me in and brought my covers up to my waist. Then each one kissed me on my forehead, but not where Aunt Ellen had placed the mud.

Aunt Ellen went back to the bureau where she turned off the cassette player and took the incense sticks to the sink to extinguish them. Dad and Azalea waited for her by the door. Someone turned off the light and all three stepped out of the motel room and left me there to sleep and, as Hamlet said, "perchance to dream."

I don't know if it was the visit to Mom's grave, all the stops on the drive south, the ceremony Aunt Ellen had just conducted, the glass of water Dad gave me to wake me up at night, or all of those things combined. Whatever it was, I had two dreams and I remembered them both.

Corinne Hedden
The First Dream

In the first dream I found myself drifting above a waterfall and realized it was Buttermilk Falls. I wasn't seeing it as I had when we visited the scene. Instead, I was looking over it as if I was a spirit. I was back in time and could see myself as a child stuck out on the stones. My mother was there, walking onto the stones the way she had on the day she died. She was dressed in the same white blouse and long yellow skirt she had worn that tragic afternoon.

There was water falling from above us as well as below. The speed of the Raquette River was magnified as the water tumbled down the mountain of stones. It was like a tsunami, hitting the slim ankles of her dancer legs. She picked up the hem of her skirt to prevent the material from catching the deluge but the water was too powerful and the stone she stood on was like ice.

She went down, hitting her knee, rolling over, hitting her shoulder and finally hitting her head as she fell into the rush of water that pushed her over the steepest cliff. Her blood poured out, then washed away almost immediately. Her arms were flailing as if she was still alive but it was the water pushing them this way and that. Her skirt hung on a branch caught in one of the crevices between two rocks. I found myself hoping, wishing, praying, that she would hold on to that log somehow and pull herself to safety. Instead her skirt ripped off her and she tumbled down further, bouncing five more times on rocks until she finally landed at the base of the falls in a pool of water. She was face down with her back up, the water spinning around her as if she was caught in a whirlpool. Her soaked hair was dark.

I wanted to see her face and somehow this prayer

was answered—unlike the prayers I'd shouted out as she was falling to her death. My dream pulled me down into the pool. I looked up to see the blank, wet face of my drowned mother. Her eyes were open but had rolled up into her head. I knew it was her because I'd seen her fall but she was too mangled to be recognizable.

I woke and I was shaking. I got up and went to the bathroom. I thought I was going to be sick to my stomach but all I did was pee. After I was done there, I looked at the clock to see it was only a little after two in the morning. That dream was horrible. I knew I couldn't tell anyone about it. It would only bring more misery to my dad and to Aunt Ellen.

Since that could not have been a message from Mom and I still needed one, I followed my dad's instructions, drank another whole glass of water, slipped into bed and started to recite the first phrase of the Lord's Prayer, *Our Father Who Art in Heaven*, over and over again. This message had to get through to God and to Mom. I needed a different dream, one that could give Dad, Aunt Ellen, and Azalea some hope.

Corinne Hedden
The Second Dream

In my second dream my dad and I walked down the aisle of an old-fashion theater. We found row D, the row our seats were in. These were excellent seats, up front center. We worked our way over, awkwardly passing an elderly couple who couldn't or wouldn't stand, then took the seats that were ours. This theater was huge. The ceiling had to be a hundred feet tall, maybe more.

There was a proscenium stage and an orchestra pit filled with musicians warming up their instruments. The proscenium arch had figures of dancing elves and fairies sculpted in relief and painted gold. There was a huge, red curtain under the arch. It was closed, separating the apron from the rest of the stage. From our seats we could tell the curtain was thick, like the skin of a rhinoceros. On either side of the arch, just into the audience area, there were statues, clearly Greek or Roman but not clearly male or female.

We sat there until the conductor came out and the orchestra began to play the introductory music. The music was a weird conglomeration of 70s hits such as *Dancing Queen* and *More than a feeling* combined with classical music and Broadway tunes from *Evita* and *Les Misérables*.

The curtain opened to reveal a blank stage. Mom entered from stage right and crossed to downstage. She began to sing a Puccini aria, *Chi il bel sogno di doretta*. This was odd. She might have tried opera before she died but she wasn't a fan. I don't remember her singing arias around the house.

Mom spun about and began to dance. She never left the stage but although she had been wearing a floor-length

Elizabethan dress she was now in white tights, a white leotard with ruffled sleeves, and a white tutu. She went up on toe and leaped three times, crossing the entire length of the stage. Each time the motion of her body was defined by her arms, as she gently raised and then lowered them. After that she held herself up on her left foot as she kicked her right repeatedly, then spun around and repeated the move from the other side. After a few more twirls and twists a man joined her on stage. This is when the dance became truly amazing. He lifted her and carried her across the stage, holding only her right leg. She held an upright position, then suddenly draped herself across his shoulder, her upper body facing down against his back with her arms around his waist. He held her with one hand on her hip while she pointed one leg up and the other down.

I looked closer at the man, who seemed to have superhuman strength. That's when I saw this dancer was my dad. He'd come into the theater with me so this surprised me. I turned to my right to see Azalea sitting two seats away from me. There was a young boy between us. I leaned over and asked, "Who are you?"

He smiled and said, "*Ciao. Mi chiamo Pietro.*"

He was dressed in medieval clothing: brown leggings, a loose, light brown shirt, and a dark brown, long vest. He had leather wraparound shoes and a leather hat that fit over his head like a glove. I had no idea what he was saying, but somehow I knew who he was. This was the person who once had the soul meant for Azalea's baby. He had been in Italy during the Middle Ages. I smiled at Azalea who grinned back. I'd known her my entire life and had never seen her so happy.

I turned back to the stage to see my parents standing there looking directly at me. Mom was now dressed in a white, long sleeve blouse, and a yellow, maxi skirt. She had on sunglasses and a straw hat. I recognized this outfit. It was what she had worn the day she died at Buttermilk

Falls. Dad was dressed in jeans and a red university T-shirt with the words 'It's Always SUNY in Ulster' written across his chest.

"We were meant to be together," they said in unison, "all of us."

"But you died, Mom! We aren't together!"

Dad had his arm around Mom while he looked at me. He laughed and said, "Yes, we are."

"It's all good," Mom said.

At that moment I remembered why they were in my dream and why I was there with them. We'd come all this way to learn Mom's plans for my life.

"What should I do?" I asked her.

"Sing and dance."

"You told me Neil would drop me," I yelled. "What else do I need to know?"

She smiled, grabbed Dad's hand and said what I thought was, "Love your father," although her words might have been, "*I* love your father."

This wasn't the clear answer I'd been looking for. They turned from the audience, crossed to the left-wing of the stage and exited. Dad had his arm around her waist as they walked.

I called out, "Wait! I don't understand! What should I do?"

They didn't respond. I woke before I could ask again. I needed to pee so badly I would have wet the bed if I'd waited any longer.

St. Joseph's Oratory
On the Steps #3

Gregory could only crawl up a few more steps. He was feeling stomach pains again, but it was the exhaustion that slowed him. The climb was taking more effort than he had thought it would but he wouldn't give up when he was so close.

"What kind of a future life would you want if you could have anything?" Corinne asked once he was seated in a position where he could rest. "You said you wanted more time with me but what else? I mean, imagine any life you can dream of no matter how impossible it sounds—your personal paradise."

"No pain, right?"

Corinne's eyes lit up. "Of course, no physical or emotional pain."

"That's fairly simple." He smiled. "I'd want to go back to Woodstock but this time I'd want everyone I have loved with me."

"Would we all be the same age?"

"I guess so—all at twenty-three, give or take a couple of years. I suppose that's about the perfect age, old enough to know some things but not so old life has settled into a routine. Your mother was eighteen when I met her but I would make her a little older."

Corinne sat up straight and leaned toward her dad. "Who do you want there with us?"

"Your Aunt Ellen, of course," Gregory answered, laughing. "She was there the first time and I would want her back. I suppose we could throw in Bobby and Tim. They were with me when I met your mother. You don't know Tim. He was fun."

"How about drugs?"

Gregory's head jerked back.

"Come on, Dad. This is Woodstock you're talking about and I know about Aunt Ellen's history."

"No. No drugs," he said, shaking his head. "The music, the camping and the wonderful, crazy people were enough. Besides, I like the second version of Aunt Ellen best, the one that looks for life's big picture through spiritual rather than chemical means."

"So do I," Corinne agreed, her voice sounding bubbly, "and I never knew the first version. Still, Woodstock with no drugs and lots of religion sounds more like a tent revival than a rock festival."

"Maybe so, but I never heard of a revival with Jimi Hendrix, Janis Joplin, and Country Joe McDonald."

They both laughed.

"How about you?" Gregory asked. "Tell me about your heaven. That is what we're describing, right?"

Corinne rubbed the back of her neck and furrowed her brow slightly before saying, "I think I'd want to be on a stage somewhere. That's where I've been most comfortable. I'd want to be singing a great song with lots of emotion like *Somewhere* from *West Side Story* but I would want you there with me, along with everyone I love, just like what you want. Only I'd want all of you to sing harmony. I see the best parts of my life as choral numbers rather than solos."

"I suppose that's true for most of us."

Corinne nodded. "Do you want to climb some more steps?"

"Alright."

***

Gregory was breathing heavily. They stopped to rest again. This time he held his head up and looked around as they sat on the steps. Corinne saw what he was doing and joined him. She put her hand on her father's shoulder and twisted so she could see up the stairs where he was looking. "The man with one leg is gone, and so is the woman wearing the hijab."

Gregory smiled. "It appears we are the slowest climbers."

Corinne nodded. Everyone was passing them, reaching the goal and moving on.

"What do you think happened to the one-legged man?" she asked.

"I don't know. I didn't see him reach the top." Gregory lifted his hands, palms up and shrugged. "If his leg suddenly reappeared I'm sure there would have been a lot of yelling and screaming." He narrowed his eyes. "The fellow must have left unsatisfied."

Corinne put her palms together and raised them to her lips. "That doesn't mean God didn't hear his prayers," she said, as much to herself as to her father.

"It does mean he didn't get the answer he wanted."

"Maybe God will connect him with someone who can give him an artificial leg. Who knows?" She turned to her father. "Are you ready to move again?"

"Give me a few minutes more."

They looked at the others who were now climbing beside them. One was an extremely skinny young woman dressed in jeans and a denim jacket. Even through her loose jacket they could tell she was anorexic. "Her problem seems like the kind God can handle," Gregory commented.

"God can handle any problem," Corinne answered, "but you have to believe. Climbing the steps is an act of faith. That's what is important. If you're climbing for some reason that has nothing to do with God, He will know."

"Some other reason?"

"You can't be here just to please me. You have to want to be better."

"Not always," someone said to them. They

recognized the voice. Gregory and Corinne turned as one and there was Reverend Adcock from the United Methodist Church in Saugerties, standing on the other side of the banister separating the tourists from the pilgrims. He looked for all the world like an angel of the Lord. "God knows our faith," he said, "but He also knows the faith of those around us. Their prayers are often the ones He answers."

"What are you doing here?" Gregory asked.

"I'm here to say you are loved by many people, people who are praying for you. Their prayers and yours, Corinne, may be enough even if you, Gregory, have lost your faith. When Lazarus was raised from the dead it was his sisters, Mary and Martha, who had the faith."

"But how did you know we were here?"

"When I first heard of your plans I thought I would support you by leading the congregation in prayer at our services and by encouraging everyone to pray at home. Then I decided that wasn't enough. I needed to demonstrate my own faith in God's miracles, so I came here."

"You still haven't answered my question." Gregory pointed at the reverend. "How did you know we were here? Did Cyn speak to you?"

He smiled but shook his head. "There was no message from the afterlife. I heard of your plans from Ellen. Still, God led me here but in other, more subtle ways. I felt His calling. It was like a wave pushing me toward you, not a tidal wave but a gentle one, the type you might find on the river on a calm day."

"So what now?"

"I'm here to tell you to keep praying, kissing, and climbing. I'll follow and speak with you the next time you stop to rest."

***

The other climbers were still passing Corinne and her

father, but when they stopped to rest one more time, Reverend Adcock was there, pulled along like the line of a fisherman trolling after a boat.

"I have something personal to tell you," he said before either Corinne or Gregory could speak. "It's about my own miracle and the reason I am who I am. Would you like to hear?"

Corinne blinked a couple of times and looked at her father. He was sitting up tall, staring at Reverend Adcock. She nodded and the reverend smiled.

"When I was a teenager with only a year's driving experience, I was heading down a hill on the Taconic State Parkway. It was raining, not pouring, but a light sprinkle as constant as a river's flow kept the surface wet. I had good tires but I was driving too fast for the slippery slope. My car hydroplaned, spun around, and I found myself praying as I was heading for a truck coming up the road toward me. Then, like a scene change in a film, I was suddenly at the bottom of the hill, safely parked at the side of the road.

"I explained this to my parents after I was home. They said memory loss was common after such a traumatic event. Maybe they were right. Perhaps I somehow saved myself and forgot everything between losing control of the car and pulling to the side of the road. However, I choose to believe God granted me a miracle and in gratitude for what happened that day I became a minister."

"Is that why you followed us here?" Gregory asked him. "To tell us that?"

"It's one of the reasons."

"What is another reason?" Corinne asked in a soft voice.

"I love you both and want to do everything I can to help." Everyone was silent for a moment until Reverend Adcock asked, "May I pray with you?"

After they prayed together Corinne and Gregory kissed the step and started climbing again. Reverend

Adcock followed.

***

When they stopped Reverend Adcock excused himself and walked up the tourist steps toward the top.

"Where's he going?" Corinne asked.

"Not sure but I imagine he's looking for a restroom."

Corinne hesitated. "Speaking of which." She furrowed her brows before asking, "Are you doing okay with that?"

Gregory wrinkled his nose. "Per your suggestion I wore an adult diaper to take care of it."

"Then I guess we're both protected."

He muttered, "Can we talk about something else?"

Corinne grinned. "Sure. Are you feeling pain?"

"I always feel some, but not much right now."

"Good."

"I wonder why God designed us to have so many problems, especially as we age."

She bit her cheek before saying, "I suppose life is a test of our faith and strength."

"Maybe so." *Or a wound that won't heal.*

Corinne pushed her hair out of her face. "If God gave you a second chance, is there anything you would have done differently?"

"If I could go back and stop the accident that took your mom I'd do that, of course, but I get the feeling that's not what you're asking?"

She nodded. "I mean smaller things—life's choices. Do you ever wish you had kept up with your studies, got a degree and became a scientist or a teacher?"

"I'm happy with where I live and what I do day to day. How about you?"

"I would not have agreed to do the play that hurt you, but I'm pleased with all my other decisions."

"Then I guess we need to reach the top of the stairs, right?"

"Just a little further, maybe twenty-five to go. You ready?"

They started to climb once more.

***

Gregory had to stop again. He looked up. There were ten, maybe twelve steps to go. They were making great progress but he needed more rest. He felt like a marathon runner who had turned the last corner and could finally see the banner marked *FINISH*.

"Are you in pain?" Corinne asked again.

"I'm just tired, very tired." He started to shake as if he had Parkinson's but he didn't. He had to get his mind off his exhaustion or he wouldn't be able to go on. He looked at Corinne whose jaw had dropped as she watched him shiver. "I was wondering what you think the future holds for us?" he asked her. "If this miracle occurs?"

"I think you'll go on living for another twenty years or so."

"But what will my life be like?" He let out a breath he didn't know he was holding. "I don't want to leave Libra Park, not completely. I know I've spent a lot of time with you in Manhattan over the years but I've kept up with my work there. I've had a good life and there are so many memories with both you and your mother. I love all the people who depend on me. Yet I understand that you can't move there. Your career depends on you being in Manhattan where the auditions are. Still, I want to be sure I spend time with you. Does the future mean I keep splitting my time?"

Corinne raised her eyebrows. "Is that so bad?"

"Not now but eventually I'll be in the way."

"You'll never be in the way. Let's keep on climbing. We'll worry about what comes next after we

convince God to save you."
***

"Blech!" Gregory spit off to the side, under the banister to where the tourists walked. He didn't want to spit where another pilgrim might kiss.

"What is it?" Corinne asked.

"I didn't look before I kissed the step this time and something got in my mouth, a bug of some sort. I hate that feeling. It was like biting into a rotten peach." He spit again and wiped his mouth with the back of his hand.

"Did you say the prayer?"

"No. I was too busy emptying my mouth."

"Then kiss the step again and say the prayer the way we've been doing it all along. You can't miss even one step."

Gregory sighed and pressed his lips to the wood and said, "Help me, Lord. Help me get past this cancer that's wrecking my body. Please Lord, please. I need more time with my daughter, for thine is the kingdom, and the power, and the glory, forever. Amen."

Corinne gave her father a curt nod. "Are you ready to move on?"

"Yes."
***

"Corinne! Gregory! I'm back." Reverend Adcock waved his arms at the two climbers. He had returned to his position standing on the tourist steps on the other side of the banister. "I stopped at the top to look at you two praying and climbing. You are amazing. I hope you realize that. In a way the miracle you're seeking has already occurred. There's no miracle greater than love and yours is evident in every step you climb." His legs were straight and his chin was high.

"We're trying to save Dad's life," Corinne replied,

her jaw clenched. "I can't stand the thought of losing another parent. I need you to pray his cancer will be gone once we reach the top. We're after the real miracle. That's why we're here and we need you to have faith it will happen. We do not need some silly excuse for failure."

Gregory was now having to stop at each step and rest for a minute or two. The pain in his stomach was back and he'd soiled the adult diaper he'd worn. The steps they were climbing had become the sheer cliff of a mountain and whenever they moved he felt as if he was losing his grip. Still, he could finish this with Corinne beside him. He took in another breath and started to twist into the position to climb again.

Corinne stopped him with a hug. "Rest a little more. There's no need to rush. God will hear us no matter how long it takes."

They sat together for a few minutes more, studying the beauty of the buildings beneath them, the grass in front of the basilica and the surrounding buildings.

"Our Father," Reverend Adcock called out. "Be with these two children of yours. Help them reach their goal. Help them honor You!"

Gregory and Corinne looked at the reverend, nodded to him, then turned and climbed one more step.

***

"Are you alright?" Reverend Adcock asked Gregory after he and Corinne had climbed six more steps.

"I'm fine," he said, although the muscles in his legs and arms were extremely sore. "I'm tired and I have some pain in my stomach but I've made it this far and I intend to finish." He rubbed his eyes before he added, "I wonder about you being here. What do you normally do when a parishioner is sick and out of town?"

"I try to go wherever God needs me. Generally, the only thing required is a trip to the hospital along with my patience and prayer, but I have driven to Massachusetts and Connecticut when people needed me in those states."

"That's not quite as far as Canada."

"No, it's not. Still, I'm here to support you and, as I said before, you are symbolically important not only to the members of our church but to all who might hear of your efforts. Miracles happen when people believe."

Gregory thought it was outrageous to travel so far just to watch something that might not happen. He massaged his stomach. "People die every day," he told the reverend, "and this might be my day." He took in a breath. "If that happens what will you tell the faithful?"

"Do you feel you're dying?"

"I'm exhausted and in pain."

Corinne held her hand up to stop them from speaking. "You're fighting to live," she told her father. Her soft voice pulled him from his pain like a narcotic and his panic dissolved.

He smiled and so did Reverend Adcock who noticed the change.

Gregory turned back to him. "I heard Cyn's voice earlier. She told me to come to her. What do you think that means?"

"I'm only human. I don't know what God is thinking or what message your wife is sending from her place in heaven but I know our souls are eternal and we will all be together again."

Gregory remembered Ellen's words at his wedding but asked, "And as for now?"

"As for now we just keep trying."

Gregory nodded. Reverend Adcock prayed again for God's healing power, then Corinne and her father resumed the climb.

Gregory Hedden
A Professional Actress

We didn't get exact information from Corinne's dream. We spent the entire trip back from Greensboro analyzing it. The question Corinne had thrown out to her mother was, "What should I do?" Cyn's answer was once again, "Sing and dance." After all that effort we had no more than what we had when five-year-old Corinne heard her mother's voice speaking to her from a sandcastle church.

Or did we?

The dream told Azalea that a young boy from medieval Italy had possessed the soul intended for her baby. Yet her pregnancy was at most an embryo, nowhere near becoming a fetus. How could it have had a soul? Corinne's other dream had proven that Cyn knew the future. Could this soul have been one that will end up in a baby born to Azalea much later in her life? Ellen made that suggestion and the idea seemed to please Azalea.

Then there was my role in the dream. I walked into the theater with my daughter but somehow ended up on stage with my wife. Was there symbolism to that? Was I to move from the world of my daughter to the world where Cyn existed?

I was carrying Cyn with one hand. I'm not a weak man but there is no way I could do that. Perhaps it was symbolic. Maybe this dream was tied back to the other dream of Corinne's. Neil dropped her. I did not drop Corinne's mother. When Cyn said, "We were meant to be together," did that mean our marriage does not end at death? And when she added "all of us" did that mean our family does not end at death?

The drive from Greensboro to Saugerties took us

over eleven hours, which included stopping a couple of times for lunch and dinner. Along the way, we talked about nothing other than Corinne's dream. We came up with hundreds of possible answers but there were only a few we were sure about. First, we were certain Cyn's soul was out there. Death was not the end. Second, she was speaking to Corinne through this dream. This was not some trick Corinne's subconscious mind was playing on us. The initial dream was real. We had proof of that because its predictions came true. Finally, even though Cyn spoke to Corinne, we knew her messages were to all of us. She said, "We were meant to be together, all of us." And she included Azalea in the dream. Her connection with Corinne was the strongest but she cared for us all.

When we pulled into the driveway beside our house in Saugerties we sat there for a moment until I said, "Where do we go from here?"

Ellen steepled her hands and brought them to her mouth. "We take one day at a time and always keep the dream in the back of our minds. Someday we will know the answers."

That's what I did and what Corinne did as well. She told Bobby she wanted to work with Donna Taylor who arranged a role for her within a month after they signed the agent contract. The part was Debbie in a production of *The Real Thing* by Tom Stoppard, a small but important part. The odd thing was the show wasn't a musical so she wouldn't be singing and dancing. I was concerned about that but Corinne convinced me this part would lead to others.

Corinne moved out of our home and into Bobby's apartment in Manhattan. She had to move to New York to get to the theater each night. Bobby didn't stay there very often. When he wasn't in a touring show he was usually in Saugerties with Neil and Ellen. When he had to stay in the city for an audition or was cast in a New York play,

Corinne had to give up the bedroom and sleep on his couch. Since Corinne had grown up in our commune, she was used to living with other people and Bobby had been staying at our house in Libra Park off and on for years. It might seem odd to allow my sixteen-year-old daughter to share an apartment with a man in his thirties, but I trusted him.

The apartment they shared had a single bedroom with a small bath and a hall connected to a sitting room. Along the hall there was a small counter, a sink, a refrigerator, and a stove. This was a hall, not a kitchen, but it served the purpose. There was a table in the sitting room where she could eat her meals but there were also a couple of upholstered chairs, a couch and a television so she could relax or entertain a friend or two. The situation worked out well for Bobby and Corinne. We now covered half the rent which was a relief to him.

She still wanted to get her high school diploma so officially we started homeschooling her. I drove to Manhattan once or twice a week to help her with her studies but she did most of the work herself.

Meanwhile, I focused on a single takeaway I had from the trip to North Carolina. If Cyn could connect with Corinne then she could connect with me. I decided to start attending the church where Corinne had first heard Cyn's voice. I hoped the location would help her reach out. I also hoped getting to know other people who believed souls are eternal would help me reach out to her.

As the years went by my involvement with the church increased. I joined their building and grounds committee and, with Phyllis' help, started a vegetable garden in a patch of land along Post Street. We allowed people in Saugerties to come help with the harvest when the season was right. Anything they picked they could take home to their families.

I enjoyed the service work but I didn't give up on my desire to reconnect with my wife. I went to Sunday

Service early every week and spent about fifteen minutes sitting in a pew, praying to Cyn, hoping she would send a sign. I also went by the church at least two times a week to sit on the front stoop and pray to the wind chimes, the ones that had called to Corinne.

Corinne and I called each other regularly. When she was young we spoke three or four times each week. The long-distance charges were enormous but well worth it. I was on the phone with her when she celebrated landing some good roles, including my favorite, Mary Jane in *Big River*. I drove down to see her five times and every time she performed *You Oughta Be Here with Me* the audience went crazy for her.

I never stopped doing the things I was supposed to do as Corinne's father. I consoled her when she broke up with boyfriends. I even listened to her cry over the phone the time one of them broke up with her (even though I was glad to see that one go). But those relationship issues stopped after she was cast in a production of *Dutchman* by Amiri Baraka. Corinne was twenty-eight by this time and cast alongside a twenty-one-year-old actor named Jim Konar. The script required a thirty-year-old white woman (Corinne) to manipulate, tease, pretend to seduce, and eventually kill a young black man (Jim).

At first I thought it was a bad idea for Corinne to accept the role. I didn't like the violence plus there was no singing and the only dance was erotic, so all that seemed to go against the instructions from Cyn. However, it came at a time when Corinne wasn't cast in another show and it paid well. It turned out to be the best role she'd ever had because Jim Konar was a wonderful person: charming, funny, thoughtful, and enthralled by my daughter. They started seeing each other off stage and in less than a year Corinne moved out of Bobby's apartment to live with her boyfriend.

I talked to Corinne about church and encouraged

her to find one in the city. She said the theater kept her too busy, but I think the real reason was her experience with Neil had soured her on organized religion. Jim, however, had attended a Baptist church when he was young. He hadn't been in a church in years, but he picked up on my encouragement. Soon, he and Corinne were attending Trinity, an Episcopalian church on the corner of Wall Street and Broadway. Jim had a beautiful voice, almost as good as Corinne's. I suspected they chose Trinity because of the excellent choir. They both sang in it when their time permitted.

I saw *Dutchman* five times before the production closed. Twice the three of us had drinks after the show, but Jim and I didn't talk much.

"He's so much fun," Corinne would tell me over and over again. Yet the first time I had a chance to talk with him alone was when I drove to the city to celebrate her twenty-ninth birthday. Corinne ran into a friend at Rosemary's, the west village restaurant where we'd gone for dinner. She left our table and went to speak to this other actress for at least ten minutes. Jim and I were left alone while they compared career notes.

I was a little nervous because I had witnessed Jim being killed on stage by my daughter in a play that speaks to racial hatred. Now they were living together. I knew enough not to judge actors by the characters they play and even if I had, Lulu, the woman in *Dutchman*, was the insane one. The character Jim played was simply a naive, young black man. Yet I had to ask the question, "Why did you choose the part of Clay?"

He shrugged. "I heard about the role and auditioned. That's all there was to it. I go to many auditions and take the parts I can get. Actors who aren't well known can't be too picky." He furrowed his brow. "But the play is good. It makes people think."

I nodded and we were both quiet for a moment.

Jim slid his chair closer to mine. "Is that the real question on your mind or are you actually wondering why I'm dating your daughter?"

"You're living with her," I pointed out. "That's a bit more than dating. But I can see how much you care in the way you look at her."

Corinne came back to our table before I mentioned I could also tell she cared for him. It wasn't important because I was certain he already knew that. I ordered a bottle of Brunello, an Italian wine I had never tried. It was a risky choice but we enjoyed the food and the drink and all had a wonderful celebration.

I was pleased with the man Corinne had chosen, but it wasn't until a few months later when I heard about their roles in a new musical about missionaries in Zambia that I knew they were perfect for each other. The play was called *Mulungu*, which means God in the Nyanja language. There are some tragic scenes in the script, but overall it is an uplifting story.

Jim and Corinne broke tradition in what they chose to perform for their *Mulungu* audition and in the way they performed it. Normally actors choose a song similar to the music in the play being cast. They chose a song from a Rodgers and Hammerstein musical, which is about as distant from the African influences of *Mulungu* as possible. It is also unusual to audition with a partner because if either of the performers makes a mistake it hurts them both. But Corinne and Jim performed *Shall We Dance* from *The King and I* and were both cast.

Mulungu did not open in New York. It started in Boston then went to Toronto, Chicago, Cleveland, Pittsburgh, and Philadelphia. I saw it twice, at the first city and the last. I liked the show but the critics didn't. It didn't earn a run in New York. However, the critics and I did agree that Corinne and Jim had tremendous chemistry. *The Plain Dealer* in Cleveland said their four songs were worth the price of the tickets. What wowed me the most was that all the numbers they performed together involved singing and dancing. Cyn had to be looking down and smiling.

One other feature of Jim's made my heart pound and convinced me he was perfect for Corinne. Jim wasn't simply a black man, his skin was the darkest I'd ever seen. I associated my love for Cyn with the pure white of her complexion. Now my daughter was introducing me to the man she loved and his skin was nearly as black as charcoal.

I learned later he was of Asian descent. His parents had been born in the Tamil region of Southern India, both part of the Christian minority. They didn't know each other when they came to America. They met in Orange, New Jersey where they married and where Jim was born. Their marriage was not arranged. They chose each other, a first for both their families.

I was in awe of his skin, almost as much as I had been in awe of Cyn's when I first met her. He was like a night sky contrasted with the bright day of Cyn. If I was Cyn's sun then Corinne was James' stars, both of us part of the magic. I believe Cyn could see the balance the same way I did from wherever she was. There was something perfect, something circular, something beautiful about this mix of black and white.

I went to Ellen to ask if she ever heard of something spiritual about black and white. "It could have something to do with the Yin Yang symbol," she told me, wrinkling her nose as she spoke, "which is about blending different types of energy. Or it could be another way of stating the alpha and the omega reference in Christian doctrine. But I think we're reaching here. It seems more likely you just admire this guy and feel he's right for Corinne."

"Then why do I sense something else, something powerful."

Ellen blew her cheeks out. "You said you felt Cyn approves of this match. Could she be sending you a message? One with her feelings rather than her words?"

That was it. My hand went to my chest as I felt my blood rushing. Cyn couldn't speak to me the way she had spoken to Corinne, but she could let me know I should love this man as much as I loved our daughter.

Gregory Hedden
A Marriage Ceremony

Once Jim and Corinne moved in together I went through one of the loneliest periods of my life. That may sound odd given I was living in a commune and in the same house with my friends Ellen, Bobby, Sean, and Phyllis.

Everyone now knew Phyllis and I were a couple and our daughters accepted our relationship better than either one of us had thought they would. Our morning sessions hadn't changed much. We still had our physical relationship but now that our daughters had grown into independent young women, the problems we discussed were ours rather than theirs. Azalea and Anthony had moved to California, so Phyllis was as lonely as I was. Her eyes turned dull when I said anything about Cyn so I hadn't mentioned her name in years. Apparently, Phyllis had only known Azalea's father for a few days before he moved on. She never told me his name.

Corinne was leading a life on its own trajectory. I didn't see her at all when she was touring, which happened quite often. Even when she was in New York and Jim was on the road, she rarely had time to come to Saugerties. I would drive to see her shows when she was in New York. Sometimes we would go for a drink afterward. Jim would come along if he was available and once I brought Phyllis with me. This was all fun, but it wasn't the same as when Corinne was younger.

My life went on like this for a few years before the next big event in our lives. Corinne called me to let me know she was pregnant. She and Jim decided to get married, which happened a month before the baby was due. The wedding was performed by an Episcopal priest, a woman from Trinity church. It took place in the living room of the apartment where Jim's parents lived. Only twelve people attended, fifteen counting the bride, groom and priest.

Corinne, in deference to Jim's family traditions, wore a white sari. The dress was composed of a short sleeve top, cut short, which left her pregnant midriff exposed, and a long skirt that reached her ankles. Over the skirt and top she carried a sheer, lace drape with elegant white trim. The fabric was wrapped around her body and over her left shoulder. She held the material across her left arm. Her blonde hair had been curled and flowed gently down to just below her shoulders. She wore dark pink lipstick, subtle eyeshadow, and dark mascara. She also wore a *kundan* necklace with matching earrings and a bracelet on her right wrist. She had elaborate henna tattoos on both hands and ankles as well as a design drawn on her large belly which could be seen through the sheer drape.

Corinne had been on stage in all sorts of outfits, before and after she started to show. Yet that day she looked more beautiful than ever before, almost as wonderful as my memories of her mom. This was the woman I had raised and I was never more proud of her.

I didn't participate in the wedding because Corinne chose not to have me walk her into the room. Instead, she stood in her living room and greeted the guests as they arrived. She didn't seem at all concerned about us seeing her bridal outfit before the ceremony. When it was time for the service, the reverend waved us together. Phyllis and I took our seats in the front row.

Corinne and Jim wrote their own vows. I was impressed as they began to recite them. They were both actors, accustomed to adding expression to their memorized words. But this was different. These words were their own, straight from their hearts to our ears.

Jim was the first to speak. "For a long time I

wondered if I would ever meet a woman I could love. Most of my friends are people I've met in various shows I've been in. When the runs were over we would try to stay in touch but our careers pushed us to go separate ways. Then I won the part in *Dutchman*, where I found myself acting across from the most giving, loving, and talented woman I'd ever met. Even before the play opened I knew I could not let you get away. It feels wonderful to have a future with you as my life partner and to look forward to raising our child. Your voice is beautiful whether you are singing alone or in harmony with me. And the same is true of your soul. You are also a perfect dance partner. On the dance floor, holding you in my arms, I discovered we move as if we are one person. I've never felt that before and that beautiful unity extends to our life off stage as well. When we dance we seem to know what each other is thinking and how we are about to move. I love that about you but even more I love how you've translated it to all of the life we share. You are beautiful, inside and out. I want to be with you always. I promise to love you not just until death do us part, but forever."

Corinne smiled at Jim and began her own vow. "We met in the most unusual of ways. I was playing a character who tries to seduce you, then kills you. I can't imagine any of our friends having such a strange beginning to their relationships. But what I learned when we weren't on stage was that you are a total professional. You are always concerned about your art and that concern extends to my art as well. You supported me when I needed it and you became a person I could go to for advice about the rest of my life. I'm talking about the confusing part where the lines aren't written for me. I found your inner warmth and strength to be beyond what I had expected I could find in a man. My love for you grew every day and now we are setting off on our newest path. Our life together and…" She glanced down at her belly for a moment then returned her gaze to Jim's eyes. "...our greatest creation. We will teach this child and watch as she becomes the most fantastic person she can be." Corinne paused again. "I also promise to love you forever, Jim Konar. I love your creativity, your kindness, your intelligence, and your loyalty—and it doesn't hurt that you're handsome."

We all laughed at her tagline. I enjoyed their words and could see they were perfect for each other. The one surprise in Corinne's vow was when she referred to her baby as "she." I'd been hoping for a girl, but they had not told me my prayers had been answered.

Three friends of Jim and Corinne had volunteered to sing. They performed *You Are So Beautiful, Endless Love,* and *When I Fall in Love.* I thought it was a shame there weren't more people at the wedding to hear their voices, but after the service Jim told me, "They're professionals. Plenty of people hear them sing. The size of this group is what made their performance so intimate."

"I see," I told him yet I still wished more people had been there.

After the wedding Jim's parents directed us to their kitchen where they had trays of food, American and Tamil choices. I went straight for the *Puliyodarai* and *Sambar Soru,* both vegetarian rice dishes. Phyllis, who is wary of food she doesn't know, filled her plate with the artichoke and cheese stuffed mushrooms along with ham biscuits.

Phyllis and I stayed at the reception until everyone other than our host and hostess had left. Corinne and Jim left at the same time as we did. They headed back to their apartment.

Phyllis and I also went to Manhattan. We decided to take a mini-vacation after the ceremony rather than drive back to Saugerties, so we had reserved a room in the Marriott Marquis near Times Square.

When I was with Phyllis I would close my eyes and think of Cyn. I realize that wasn't fair but it was the only way I could perform. I had never lost the ability to see the face I still ached for. I was confident Phyllis didn't know what I was doing. If Cyn's soul somehow knew, I was certain she understood.

The following day we went to the Metropolitan Museum of Art, had dinner at the Tavern on the Green and saw the Broadway production of *Les Misérables*. We stayed one more night at the Marriott before heading back to Libra Park. When we were home I dropped Phyllis off at her house. After our normal short kiss she hugged me tightly and whispered, "I had a wonderful time," before letting me go.

I started to worry her idea of what we had together might be changing. That's when I decided I wouldn't ask Phyllis to go to Manhattan with me after Corinne's baby arrived.

Corinne Hedden
A Honeymoon

It may seem odd for two actors who call New York City their home to celebrate their honeymoon in Edison, New Jersey, but that's what we did. We were taking a break from our work and to me that meant experiencing something different.

Edison was a center for Tamil people and I wanted to learn more about Jim's culture. So we took a room in the Sheraton and ate meals in Indian restaurants including Delhi Garden, Kathiyawadi Kitchen, Spice House, and Masala Bay. We also went to a Bollywood dance club called Bollywood Beats and while there we met a couple Jim hadn't seen in over fifteen years. They spoke about friends they had in common. I think my husband liked the nostalgia and I enjoyed the opportunity to learn more about him.

We had considered going big and booking a vacation in Southern India but I was getting close to my due date. We didn't want to travel too far from my doctor in New York City, especially not out of the country.

After a couple of days of immersion in Indian culture Jim told me he wanted to do something to get to know *me* better.

"I'd say you know me very well." I giggled a bit because we had just made love, an afternoon delight. We were naked, spooning in bed, one of the few positions where I could be comfortable for a long time.

He squeezed me lightly. "You know what I mean."

"I do." We'd already had this discussion. We had eaten lunch and were talking about plans for the evening. I took hold of his arm and suggested we stay in our room and do more of what we'd just done.

He moved his hand to cup my left breast. "That does sound nice but I was hoping we could do something that would be reminiscent of your background, something similar to what we've been doing for me."

I loved the warmth of his body and didn't want to leave but I gave some thought to what he was suggesting. "There is one thing," I told him, speaking softly and slowly. "We aren't far from New Brunswick. That was one of the stops we made on the trip I told you about, when Dad, Aunt Ellen, Azalea, and I went to North Carolina to visit Mom's grave."

"Are you planning to search for her spirit?" he asked, his voice trailing off as he spoke.

"Not specifically but I'm always listening and hoping. You know that. It's been a long time since I heard her voice."

"I know and that's why I don't want you to be disappointed, not ever, but especially not on our honeymoon."

"Don't worry. While I'm with you I can't be disappointed." I twisted to my back so I could look into his eyes. "We could drive over there, maybe circle by the hospital where we stopped?" Jim frowned but I continued speaking. "New Brunswick is a nice place and something is always going on at Rutgers. There could be a concert or maybe a show."

We showered, got dressed, made the fifteen-minute drive, looked over the campus, found an Italian restaurant for dinner and, as we were driving through the town, noticed that a production of *The Fantasticks* was at the George Street Playhouse. Jim had only seen that show one time. I had seen it at least five times. We parked the car and made it to the ticket window just in time.

It was a good production, well worth the ticket price. The pianist was great. My favorite song in the show is *Soon It's Gonna Rain*, sung by the two young lovers, Matt and Luisa. I closed my eyes when the song started. I listened to the gentle music and concentrated on the beautiful lyrics. That's when, just for a moment, I thought I heard Mom's voice again. I wasn't sure. It might have been an echo stuck in my head from years ago. I decided I wouldn't tell Jim. I didn't want my new husband to think I was crazy. When the show ended we applauded, followed the crowd out of the theater, found our car and headed back to Edison.

Back at the hotel we opened a bottle of Merlot and made love again. We'd been together for a while so the sex wasn't new. It was also a little awkward finding a position that worked with my huge belly. But there was something special about us now that we'd publicly professed our love and made a commitment to stay together forever.

Maybe I'd heard my mother's voice again or maybe not but this day would stay in my mind for the rest of my life and it would always be about Jim.

Corinne Hedden
Babysitting

Dad drove to Manhattan to help with the baby. I was glad he came because I was exhausted but also because I wanted him near me.

Aunt Ellen, Azalea's mom, and some of the other adults in the commune had jumped in to help when Mom died but Dad was always responsible for me. He had made all the decisions about my care, disciplined me when I needed it, went to the annual parent/teacher conferences, came to my dance shows and, although he was always busy as the fix-it guy for the commune, he managed to spend as much time as possible with me. Over the years he was always like a gentle breeze pushing me the way I needed to go.

I had told Dad his grandchild was healthy and beautiful, but there was one other important thing I had to tell him and I couldn't wait to see his reaction. He stepped into our apartment, set his luggage down in the living room, hugged me and said, "Where is she?"

James stepped out of our bedroom with the baby in his arms. He looked at Dad and, as he handed her over, he said, "Right here."

I giggled a bit, then caught my breath and said, "Dad—I want you to meet your granddaughter, Cynthia." I watched him as he realized Jim and I had named our baby after Mom. He took a step back. I could tell he was overwhelmed. He couldn't bring himself to speak but his wide eyes said everything that needed to be said.

I could see his love as he studied Cynthia's beautiful features. She didn't look like Mom. The mixture of our genes had given her beautiful, tan skin with dark black hair that had obviously come straight from her father. Her eyes were also her father's—coal-black. She would be a beauty to rival any woman.

Dad took her to the couch and sat down, rocking her. I was concerned she would cry since she didn't know him but somehow she seemed comfortable.

When she finally started to squirm a little I asked him, "Would you like to feed her?"

He nodded without taking his eyes off Cynthia.

"I'm breastfeeding, but I have some of my milk in bottles so Jim can feed her, too. You'll be using those when she gets hungry at night. She's used to both ways."

He nodded again.

Jim stepped toward him. "I can take her while Corinne shows you how to prepare a bottle."

"Where will I be sleeping?" Dad asked after he handed Cynthia to Jim and stood up.

"You'll be in Cynthia's room, but she won't be there. We're keeping her in our room so we can watch her."

"Then how are you going to sleep through the night?"

"If she wakes up Jim will get her and hand her off to you. You can feed her, change her or whatever else is needed and bring her back to the crib in our room when she settles down."

"Can you sleep through all that?"

"I believe so. I'm tired enough."

Dad stayed with us for three weeks. I don't know how I would have dealt with everything without his help. Jim was great, of course, but he received an offer for a role in a revival of *Golden Boy*. He got it through a friend and didn't even have to audition. We talked it over and since it was a major opportunity I wouldn't let him say no. He was still in New York while Dad was with us but he was busy with rehearsals and with another show that was just ending. I slept a lot for the first week but after that I was able to visit with Dad and get to know Cynthia.

I started thinking Jim was going to have a marvelous theater career while I changed from an actress to a mother. I was jealous and I guess it showed because Dad sat me down and we had a talk.

"You don't have to give up your career the way your mother did. I'm a couple of hours up the New York Thruway. I can get here anytime you need me and you can bring Cynthia there if you prefer. The three of us can raise this child together without you or Jim giving up your dreams. Your mother said you should sing and dance and that's what you should do."

"You will do that for us?"

"Of course I will and I'll have help. Phyllis and Aunt Ellen will be there. Babies require constant attention, but it doesn't have to be from one person."

I got back in shape by exercising with a morning television show and jogging with Cynthia in a running stroller. When I was ready Jim and I checked our sources and found a few shows holding open auditions. Dad came down to babysit while I went to the auditions. He brought Aunt Ellen with him.

Apparently, Azalea's mom had left for California while Dad was helping me recover from the birth. She told Aunt Ellen she wanted to spend time with Azalea and to tell Dad she wasn't sure when she would be back. They hadn't spoken since the day he left Saugerties to meet his granddaughter.

Dad wasn't sure Phyllis would ever return to Libra Park. I told him to call her, but he thought that would "give the wrong message." I had no idea what that meant and I decided not to ask. Although Dad had never been able to replace Mom with Phyllis, he seemed happy to replace Phyllis with Cynthia. He had a purpose now and a new love.

Corinne Hedden
Baptisms

Although Jim and I had been attending Trinity for nearly a year, we were not members and I had never been christened.

Mom had not wanted me to be baptized even though Dad was attending services regularly back then. The family story was that her own baptism had been traumatic. Their church performed the ritual with immersion at a small lake in Greensboro. She was eight. Mom wore a simple white dress with long sleeves and a lined skirt that reached her ankles. She also wore white tights and white shoes. She felt like an angel.

My mom had joyfully walked out into the water up to her waist, holding onto the preacher's arm. When they stopped, the man put his right hand on the back of her neck and used his left to push her over backward. She was engulfed in lake water. She had expected all this but hadn't kept her mind set right. Like someone walking a path in a forest she had concentrated on the beauty around her and had lost her way. Instead of holding her breath she inhaled. Water, not air, entered her lungs. She choked.

She was never in danger but the embarrassment of that day stayed with her for years and when the time came for my baptism, she said no—even though the ceremony would not be by immersion.

Jim and I both wanted to have Cynthia baptized so, after consulting with our minister, we decided the best course of action would be to have him baptize us both during the same ceremony.

When the day arrived, Jim and I sat in the front pew with Jim's parents and my dad in the pew directly behind us. I held Cynthia through the early parts of the service. I kept rocking her gently so she wouldn't cry. When the minister called us to the altar we stood and took our places beside the holy water font. The reverend gave a short talk about the meaning of the ritual and explained to the congregation that I would have my adult baptism prior to Cynthia's infant version. Mine would focus on my faith and beliefs. Hers on our commitment to raise her in the Christian faith.

I had on a white dress with a green, leafy pattern. It was sleeveless but I wore a jacket over it. The jacket was the same shade of green as the dress pattern. Jim wore a navy-blue suit with a white shirt and a tie halfway between the color of the shirt and the suit. Due to the ceremony we were much dressier than on most Sundays. Cynthia, however, was the most beautiful of the three of us. She had on a long, white gown with lace sleeves and matching lace over the skirt. She also wore a band of silk flowers around her head with plenty of hair showing for the sprinkling. I was so proud.

I handed Cynthia to Jim when it was time for my christening. I took a step forward and waited for the minister's questions. My part was simple. All I had to say was, "I do." The problem was the first question was unexpected.

"Do you acknowledge yourself to be a sinner, deserving God's displeasure and without hope of pardon from his mercy?"

The first part was easy. My mother's death was the greatest sin a child could commit. I had grown since then, but I still felt guilty. If that was all he had said, the words "I do" would have poured out of my mouth faster than the water that had carried Mom away on that terrible day. But that wasn't where I had the problem. The second part asked if I was "without hope of pardon from his mercy." How could I say "I do" to that?

I stood there and stared out toward the

congregation, my mouth agape until Jim said, "She does."

That wasn't good enough for our minister. He shook his head and said, "She needs to answer." He repeated the question.

"How can I answer that?" I asked. "Hope of pardon, hope of someday seeing my mother again, hope in God's mercy is all I have. All I have!"

I felt dizzy and started to swoon. Jim shifted Cynthia to his left arm and put his right around my waist.

"Are you alright?" the minister asked.

I nodded.

He let out a breath and said, "I understand. Let me rephrase the question. Do you acknowledge yourself to be a sinner in the sight of God, justly deserving His displeasure, and without hope save in His sovereign mercy?"

"I do," I answered with a quaver in my voice.

He skipped to the next question. "Do you believe in Jesus Christ as the son of God and savior of sinners and do you receive and rest in Him alone for salvation?"

"I do," I told him, speaking stronger this time.

"Do you resolve, relying on the Holy Spirit, to follow Christ as Lord of your life?"

"I do!" I told him, shouting my answer.

He turned to the congregation. "I believe God understands and accepts Corinne. Do you?"

They started applauding and some even rose to their feet. The reverend smiled. "Then we'll proceed with the baptism." He didn't just sprinkle the water on my head. He took a handful and poured it on me, then added a second handful, as if I needed a little extra to get me through life. "I now baptize you in the name of the Father, the Son, and the Holy Spirit, for the forgiveness of your sins, and the gift of the Holy Spirit."

I stepped back by Jim, with water dripping through my hair onto my jacket. I was supposed to take Cynthia back in my arms, but he wouldn't hand her over. I suppose he was scared I might still faint.

The questions for Cynthia's baptism were easier.

"James and Corinne, do you promise unreservedly to dedicate your child to God?

"We do."

"Do you promise by your example and prayer you will seek by both nurture and admonition to raise up Cynthia in the ways of the Lord, to teach her about faith in Jesus Christ, and by so ordering your own lives to have her early in life understand faith in Jesus Christ?"

"We do."

He turned to the congregation. "And you, as a church, have a commitment as well. This is not done in private. This is a community of faith. Do you promise by your prayers and by lives given in dedication to God that you also will put an example before this child so that she might, early in life, understand faith in Jesus Christ? If you so agree will you say, together, Amen?"

They shouted, "Amen."

He sprinkled a few drops on our baby's head. She didn't seem to mind at all. He took her from Jim and held her up to the congregation. They applauded again.

After the service we had coffee, tea, and snacks in the fellowship hall. Our friends and even some of the people we didn't know came up to me to tell me they understood my concern and felt the ceremony was the most moving one they had ever witnessed. One woman said, "I could tell you listened to the words and paid attention."

When I got home I thought again about my mom and her time under the water. I compared it with what I had just gone through. She was a child experiencing real fear while I was an adult living through an embarrassing moment. In that context, and given that Cynthia's ritual had been executed perfectly, the day hadn't been so bad. Still, there was something about christenings in our family that seemed to present problems. It made me wonder if God was trying to tell us something.

Corinne Hedden
An Opportunity

I didn't have much luck as I re-entered the audition process. This was strange for me because there had always been one role after another waiting around the next corner. When I was first starting out I went to some auditions where I didn't get the part but now it seemed as if I couldn't get anything.

I didn't know what it was. Perhaps my agent had too many new clients, but Donna claimed she was trying. Maybe passing thirty had cut me off from the ingenue roles and I was still considered too young for the character roles. Also, it was no secret that I'd just had a baby. I suppose the directors might have been worried about my priorities and conflicts with my time. I don't think it was my physical state. I'd lost the baby weight and I would show directors how well I could move. Yet nothing good was coming my way. I had a few offers for chorus parts but I wasn't ready to step back there. If those roles had been in major productions I might have considered them but they were all regional theater and I didn't want to leave Cynthia with Dad for an extended period. What I needed was something local that would give me a chance to prove myself again.

I was feeling quite frustrated when I received a call from Warren Lowe, a prominent director who was also a friend of a friend. He was putting together an experimental show. It would be in a small, storefront theater with a capacity for an audience of no more than fifty people. He claimed it would be a perfect showcase for my talents. He told me he was the writer, the director, and the producer, and he said he wanted to meet me for coffee to talk about it.

"I saw you in *Dutchman*," he told me as I sipped on

a vanilla latte, the first one I'd allowed myself since Cynthia was born. "I already know you'll be perfect for this role."

I was confused. *Dutchman* was years ago. "You're asking me to audition?"

"I'm saying you don't have to audition. You can have the role if you want it."

I leaned toward him excited at first, then I felt my arms start to tighten. "What's the catch?"

"There is no catch."

"This is a paying role, right?"

"Standard equity salary for off-Broadway."

I paused, tilted my head slightly, and said, "Tell me about the play."

He smiled and his eyes lit up. "It's the story of a boy whose mother died when he was five years old. The boy steps onto a road without looking. A truck is barreling toward him. His mother jumps forward and pushes him out of the way but the truck hits her and she dies."

A child who kills his mother? This was sounding too close to home.

"That all happens in the first scene. The play is centered around the boy after he has grown to be a man. He has never taken responsibility for what happened. Instead he blames God."

"You're saying he should have blamed himself? But he was a child."

"Of course he was. He still should have known better than to run onto a road without looking first. He killed his mother."

I fidgeted with the top bottom of my blouse. "Where do I come in?"

"You are an angel of the Lord. You are sent by God to convince the man to take responsibility."

I shook my head. "But he was five! Five years old!"

"That doesn't matter. God doesn't want to be

blamed for what this man did, no matter when he did it."

I shook my head. "You make God sound petty."

"Exactly. You put it so well. I knew you would be right for this show."

I wanted to turn him down. I wanted to tell him I am a Christian and walk out on him but—I needed this job. "Go on," I said.

"You attempt to seduce him, the way you did with Clay in *Dutchman* but this time you are seducing him with a utopian view, telling him he will live forever if he follows your lead, forever in a land with no problems, no troubles. Where everything works for the best."

The play sounded horrible but I told Warren I couldn't make a decision on the spot. I said I'd have to read the script first.

I needed Jim's opinion since he was the only one who would understand how important a showcase production could be for my career, especially one with Warren Lowe directing.

Jim was in the apartment with Cynthia when I got home so I sat down with him immediately. I knew enough about the play to get his opinion before I read it.

"This is something you're going to have to figure out for yourself," he told me. "Working with Warren Lowe will improve your reputation even if the show never catches on. Donna will think of you before her other clients and you'll probably get direct offers from producers. There's also the chance that Warren will keep this show moving up from showcase to Off Broadway. If that's the case this could give you work for years. But if you feel this is too much for you you're going to have to beg off. Your mental health has to take precedence over your career."

"Mental health? Are you talking about the similarity between what the boy goes through and my own experience? Because I was thinking more about the sacrilegious aspect."

He nodded at the script I was holding. "The words in the play aren't yours, even if you are the one saying them. Besides, if Warren stays with this show there's a chance he will keep changing it until it doesn't look anything like it does today. He's done that once or twice before. I don't worry about the statement the show will make as much as I worry about your ability to deal with the memories it will bring back."

"I'm stronger than you think."

"I know how strong you are. I also know you blame yourself for what happened to your mother. Warren has a reputation for looking into the backgrounds of the people he works with and using them in his projects. His idea is simple. If you understand the pain the show is portraying then you're going to give a better performance. I think that's what he's doing with you."

"But I won't be experiencing on stage what I went through in life. I'll be off to the side watching the boy go through it."

"You'll be playing God, right? Or one of his angels."

"An angel, I think, although I haven't read the script yet."

"Either way angels and gods know what's going on in our minds. That's where he wants the tension. I say read the script, evaluate how painful it will be and then make your decision."

Jim was in a show so he had to leave right after dinner. I put Cynthia down for the night at seven-thirty. After that I sat to read the play.

Warren had summed it up fairly well but it was more intense than I had expected. The boy was playing with his dog, chasing him around the area in front of his house. The dog ran into the street and the boy followed. A box truck was coming straight at them, driving at an unreasonable speed. The dog kept running, but the boy froze, his eyes wide, his body shaking. His mother sprinted into the road, grabbed her son, pushed him out of harm's way, then stumbled and fell. She died when the truck's wheels crushed her. Her death would be covered with strobe lights and sound effects.

That part wasn't unexpected. What was a surprise was how much detail in the script was given to the guilt the boy continued to feel as he grew into a man. Just like me, this boy was always dwelling on what had happened to his mother. In many ways he was worse than me. He became a loner and didn't ever try to keep friends or have relationships. He finally overcame the guilt in his mid-thirties when he met a woman who kept telling him God was in control, especially over what happens to five-year-old boys.

At the end of Act One my character makes her entrance. As Warren had said, I would be playing an angel, not God. I was relieved at that but I would still be acting in a way most Christians would consider sinful. My character's task was to split the man from the woman who had helped him. I would talk with the man, flirt with him and, after a short time, convince him to go home with me.

When the lights came up on Act Two we would both be at my place, an apartment God had set up for me. I would be dressed in a sheer, black nightgown. The man would be in his boxers with no shirt. He would watch me as I cooked breakfast. I was pleased Warren didn't have us in bed. The seduction had occurred off stage.

I took a deep breath and kept reading. I was expecting lines filled with horribly sacrilegious curses but that wasn't in the play. The most ungodlike deed, far beyond my character's seduction of the man, was God's need to pass blame, not just for the death of the mother but for all sins. The script was saying God was the one with original sin, not man. This was much worse than offensive words. The play was saying Jesus did not die for our sins.

He died for the sins of our Father. Could I be a part of that?

I needed to speak to a priest. I always told myself I had ethics. Yet even before I read the play I knew it mocked God and I was still considering it. What did that say about me? I didn't want to talk with one of the priests in our church, so I called a woman I'd known in high school. She had become a Presbyterian minister and now had a church in northern New Jersey. We reminisced for a while, but she knew I hadn't called just to talk about old times. She asked me if I had a question and I told her the decision I was facing.

She paused for a moment, then I heard a slight sigh. "You're asking me to forgive something that hasn't happened, something you're planning to do. We protestants never sold indulgences." She laughed a little at her own joke, then coughed and took in a breath. "You aren't the first person facing a dilemma like this. No matter what job you have, even the ministry, there will always be choices where your career conflicts with your faith. You have to pick your priorities and in the end you have to make the final decision yourself. God is a forgiving God no matter which way you go, but He knows if you're sincere or not."

Her words didn't solve my problem, so I called Dad and explained it all to him. This would affect him a lot. He would be sitting with Cynthia regularly. That would mean living with us or moving Cynthia up to Saugerties where Aunt Ellen could help. I imagined he would do a combination of those two options. He couldn't give up on the commune. They were still paying him to be their handyman. Maybe he would go up there a few days a week and down here the rest of the time. That would allow him to do what he had to and me to see my baby. Working mothers have it hard, especially actresses.

Dad was quiet for a while. I almost repeated myself but before I did he said, "Years ago, when Bobby and I were roommates at Rutgers, he was in a play by Samuel

Beckett called *Waiting for Godot*."

"I know the play."

"Good. Anyway, we talked about the script after I saw the show. We both agreed that it seemed to be about people who spend their lives waiting for a God who never shows up." I could hear Dad blow out his cheeks. "Bobby's a good person," he said in a quieter voice. "I never thought less of him for taking that role, even after your experience brought me back to church."

"Do you think God thought less of him?"

"I know lots of people think God is judging us every day, but I don't believe that. Other people may judge us when we make decisions they don't agree with, but the God I believe in is bigger than that."

I thought about what he said for a moment and realized I agreed with him. "So you think I should take the role?"

"I think God cares about your career and He cares about your relationship with your daughter. You need to decide how to balance those two parts of your life, then move forward. I'll support you and Cynthia whatever you decide and I'm sure God will as well."

I decided to take the role.

Gregory Hedden
Cancer

Corinne's play was successful. The critics loved it and it was still running after a couple of years. Warren Lowe decided to move it from the small, storefront theater to a one hundred sixty-seat off-Broadway theater at 555 42nd Street. Corinne was getting more exposure than ever and more invitations to auditions.

I was taking care of Cynthia who was now three years old. She went to daycare when we were in Manhattan and stayed with me and Aunt Ellen when we were in Saugerties. Cynthia would sit patiently working on her coloring book or putting together buildings with her Magna-Tile set while I did my various projects around the commune.

Everything was going well until I started feeling off. There were several signs: a dull pain in my abdomen, I was never hungry and naturally lost weight and, what bothered me the most, I was tired all the time. I decided to have a doctor check me out. She recommended a CAT scan. The news wasn't good. I had pancreatic cancer.

"I'm sorry to have to tell you this. You need to get your affairs in order."

"You're saying I'm dying?"

"Your cancer is stage four."

"How long do I have?"

"The average survival for someone with stage four is one year, although people have been known to live as long as five. It varies from case to case. I will get you signed up with a team of specialists as quickly as possible. They will start you on a regimen of chemotherapy."

The sun was setting on my life. I was scared of the

darkness that would follow but at the same time I was confident there was good in it. I would see Cyn again.

When I got back to Libra Park I spoke to Ellen. "I need to tell you something," I whispered to her. "Can I make you a cup of coffee?"

Her narrowed eyes told me she knew something serious was going on. Still, she nodded and I filled the coffeemaker. We made awkward small talk while I waited for the coffee to be ready. I didn't want to start this conversation while I was still wandering around the kitchen getting cups, milk, and sugar.

When we finally sat across from each other and each took a sip of coffee, I started to speak. The words didn't come out the first time. My nerves were pounding like the rain of a hurricane. I took a deep breath and whispered to Ellen, "I have cancer."

Her hand flew to her chest. Now she was the one who couldn't say anything. I stood, reached over and hugged her. "I know there's something after life. I'm scared but there's this other feeling inside me that wants death because Cyn's waiting for me there. I'm sure of that. But first I have a bucket list and at the top of that list is to tell you how much you've meant to me. From the time we met at Woodstock you've always been by my side. You helped me through the dark times after Cyn died and since then you've helped me every time I needed a friend."

After I told Ellen, I called Corinne. I explained that I needed to talk to her and arranged to drive to Manhattan the next day. Ellen agreed to go with me. This was hard but I couldn't put it off. If I wasn't available to take care of Cynthia, Corinne would have to make other arrangements.

The next day I talked to Corinne in her living room while Ellen grabbed Cynthia's stroller and took her out for a walk.

"This is my fault," Corinne said, her voice cracking. "I'm so sorry, so very sorry." She was starting to cry.

"I don't understand. How could you have had anything to do with this?"

"It's…the play." She was having trouble catching her breath now.

"That's ridiculous. These things happen to people all the time. It has nothing to do with anything either you or I did."

"God is punishing us for my sacrilege."

"The God I know is not a vengeful God. There has been tragedy in my life but I was blessed to know your mother and to raise you. I've loved you both and I couldn't ask for more than that. Everyone dies eventually. It's just my time."

"I knew this play was wrong yet I took the part anyway!" She was breathing hard. "I am killing you just as I killed Mom." She paused. "I need to do something."

"I don't need anything now. In fact I can still watch Cynthia for you and Ellen is a great help. You just need to find someone else to help when things get worse. Maybe you need to look into hiring an Au Pair."

"What I need to do is quit the play."

I tried to change Corinne's mind. "If you do you'll make me feel worse."

She muttered something I couldn't understand. I asked, "What did you say?"

"What you think doesn't matter," she said, stuttering a little as she spoke. Then in a stronger voice she added, "What's important is what God thinks."

I told her again how much I loved her. Shortly after that Ellen and Cynthia came back. I hugged my granddaughter and suggested she watch a movie. Corinne put *Shrek* on the TV and let her settle back to watch it while we adults moved to the kitchen.

Corinne and Ellen were both crying. "I love you," Corinne told me. "You have been a wonderful father, the best anyone could have."

"I love you also," Ellen said. "I've never known a better couple than you and Cyn. When you go I will miss you but be assured you will be with her. Your soul and hers are immortal."

Corinne Hedden
The Pilgrimage

I quit the play immediately—called Warren and told him I would never step on his stage again, not even for that night's performance. He gave me a lot of grief but it worked out fine for him. The understudy was prepared. She had been in the play for a couple of months. Her part was small and she was excited to replace me. The stage manager took her old part for a few days until they could find a replacement. I learned all this from my agent who gave me the most grief. She said it would hurt my reputation.

"I don't care. Other things are more important." I wasn't sure Mom would have agreed with what I had done but I was determined.

Dad loved Cynthia and wanted to keep watching her as much as he could. I couldn't have stopped him even if I'd tried. However, I insisted that Cynthia and I do all the traveling. Jim was still in a New York show so I decided we would go up to Saugerties three days a week and spend the rest of the week on Manhattan Island. That way Cynthia and I would have time with both of them.

Dad had his moments of pain and always seemed weak but he tried to put on a good face. Meanwhile wherever I was I made sure I didn't miss Sunday services. When I was in Manhattan I went to Trinity. When I was in Saugerties I went to the Methodist Church where I'd heard Mom's voice. It didn't matter to me what type of service I attended as long as I could talk to God and tell Him how sorry I was, how my priorities were all wrong. "I'll do anything to save Dad," I prayed over and over again.

I listened to my own words and was soon

researching miracles because that's what we needed. I found a few places around the country where miracles had been recorded: St. Joseph Maronite Church in Phoenix, Arizona, where a blind woman had been cured, The Shrine of St. John Berchmans in Grand Coteau, Louisiana where a young novice of the Society of the Sacred Heart was healed and The Shrine of St. Joseph in St. Louis, Missouri where a dying man was healed after he kissed a relic of St. Peter Claver. But I believed we needed to demonstrate to God that I was truly repentant and that Dad wanted to live. When I read about St. Joseph's Oratory in Montreal Canada, I knew that was where we had to go. If we climbed and kissed those ninety-nine steps together, God would help us.

St. Joseph's Oratory
On the Steps #4

Gregory and Corinne moved to the step preceding the top and kissed it. One more climb and they would reach their goal.

Gregory said his prayer, changing the words from the ones he had recited on the other steps. Instead of saying, "...Help me get past this cancer that's wrecking my body. Please Lord, please. I need more time with my daughter and granddaughter..." he said, "Thank you, God, for giving me the strength to make this climb. I ask for your will to be done. I love Corinne and Cynthia and also Jim. I am so grateful that You allowed her to find him. Yet Corinne needs to live her life with her husband and her daughter and to move on from the life I gave her when she was a child. Please help her do that. If I need more time on this planet to help the people I love then grant that to me but if I could just be with Cyn one more time to hold her and to allow our hearts to merge again, that would be how I see heaven. Cyn will always be my life and my heart."

Gregory got to his knees and put forth one last effort to climb the step. As he moved up he became dizzy. He collapsed half on the step he was leaving and half on the landing he was trying to reach. He seemed to leave his body, floating up over the steps. He was consumed in clouds for a moment and when he was able to look down again he wasn't over St. Joseph's Oratory. He was staring at a soft grassy spot in a cluster of trees near the Woodstock Festival. There were two naked bodies below him.

It took Gregory a few seconds to realize he was seeing himself as a teenager, lying on his back with Cyn curled up next to him, her head on his chest. They were both asleep, at least that's what he first thought, but as he floated closer he saw Cyn carefully separating from him. His teenage self stirred but fell back asleep. She removed her arm from around his waist and leaned forward and kissed his lips so gently she didn't wake him. The crescent moon provided enough limited light to move about. However, Gregory's spirit could see perfectly.

Cyn scrounged for her clothes. They were scattered but she finally found her bra and panties not too far from the green dress, hat, socks, and sneakers she'd had on before they'd made love. She slipped into her clothes as carefully and silently as she could. She turned away, took a few steps, then turned back.

Gregory's spirit could hear her thoughts as she stared at his teenage body breathing deeply. She remembered holding him. She remembered kissing him. She thanked God for the time they had together and said a prayer that they might meet again. She wanted to wake him but knew she wouldn't be able to leave if she did. Instead she went to where the car was parked and Ellen was waiting.

Gregory's spirit was suddenly back in his body, lying on the steps. He raised his head, looked up and saw a woman's legs. He thought for a moment he was still at Woodstock but back at a point earlier in the day when he'd first met Cyn. Then he looked higher and saw they belonged to a stranger. The woman backed away and Reverend Adcock took her place. That's when Gregory realized where he was.

"Are you alright?" Reverend Adcock asked as he knelt down in front of the two pilgrims.

Gregory nodded and finished the last climb to the top of the steps.

"Dad," Corinne cried to him. "You made it. This will work. You will heal."

He twisted around to sit at the top of those long

stairs and looked back at what he had accomplished.

Corinne reached out and touched his cheek. "Life may be a struggle at times," she told her dad, "but the future you earn is forever." She wore a smile as wide as the steps he'd just climbed.

"Amen to that," Reverend Adcock said.

Cynthia Hedden-Konar
Epilogue

After the climb at St. Joseph's, my grandfather's cancer went into remission. It came back and he died when I was twelve but we had many happy years together. When Mom, Dad, and I would visit the commune he would often take us to Saugerties Village Beach where we would swim in Esopus Creek, a tributary of the Hudson River. He said there was another nice place to swim further upstream in the Mohonk Preserve, but it was near a waterfall and my mom told us we weren't allowed anywhere close to that.

I learned to ride a bike in Saugerties. Dad tried to teach me in Manhattan but the streets were too busy and the sidewalks were crowded. He took me to Washington Square once, but there were too many people there as well. So he decided we'd visit Gramps on a couple of Mondays and bring the bike with us each time. That worked well. Dad did the balancing and running alongside me, but I still remember Gramps cheering me on.

He missed many wonderful events in my life, the ones that occurred after he had passed: my high school and college graduations, my first job as an engineer with Lockheed Martin, my marriage to Aaron, the birth of our daughter, Poppy. Mom and Dad were there for all of those along with Patti and Tatta, my grandparents on my father's side, but I always missed Gramps.

Aunt Ellen assured me he was out there watching us. Each time I would go through one of those milestones she would tell me the old stories about Gramps and Cyn, the grandmother I never met. I didn't really believe all those stories, especially the one about the miracle. I know his cancer went into remission but that could have happened without their pilgrimage. There are many cures coming up every day because doctors and scientists are working to end the plague of cancer.

I believed they met at Woodstock and I found that story kind of fun. But Gramps living years beyond the time the doctors had given him because he traveled to Montreal and climbed ninety-nine steps? I had trouble with that.

Then I brought Poppy to meet a friend in Haddonfield at Mountwell Park. The girls were playing in a sandbox and I decided I'd help. Together we built a small, sand town with lots of homes connected by winding roads. I declared one of the mounds to be a church. I made a cross out of a couple of twigs which I bound together with some Scotch tape I had in my purse. When the town was complete, the girls and I sat at the edge of the sandbox admiring our work.

Now—I wouldn't admit this if I'd been the only one, but it's true. We were quiet for a couple of minutes as we looked over what we had accomplished. That's when we *all* heard a voice we were certain had come from the sand church. The voice said, "Sing and dance."

I've attended church all my life. I love the friendships, the music, and the shared rituals. Yet it wasn't until after I heard the voice that I knew for sure I will see Gramps again and, when I do, I'll meet the soul of the beautiful woman behind that voice, my grandmother.

About Steve Lindahl

Woodstock to St. Joseph's is Steve Lindahl's seventh novel. His first three, *Motherless Soul, White Horse Regressions,* and *Hopatcong Vision Quest* are historical fiction stories wrapped in modern mysteries. In these books, the characters must look into their past life memories to find clues concerning crimes in the present. His fourth and fifth books, *Under a Warped Cross* and *Living in a Star's Light,* are also historical novels, but without the regression twist. *Under a Warped Cross* is set in the tenth century, in Scandinavia, Ireland, and Britannia. *Living in a Star's Light* follows the life of Lotta Crabtree, a nineteenth-century actress who achieved great fame and wealth. His sixth novel, *Chasing Margie,* is the story of Margie, a young girl from an extremely wealthy family who goes missing in the early twentieth century and Sarah, a twenty-first-century woman of very modest means, who discovers she is descended from the missing girl and from the girl's fortune. Steve's short fiction has appeared in *Space and Time, The Alaska Quarterly, The Wisconsin Review, Eclipse, Ellipsis,* and *Red Wheelbarrow.*

Steve served for five years as an associate editor on the staff of *The Crescent Review,* a literary magazine he co-founded and he is currently the Managing Editor of *Flying South,* a literary magazine sponsored by Winston-Salem Writers. He loves to read as much as he loves to write and has posted hundreds of reviews on Amazon, Goodreads, Librarything, and his blog (www.stevelindahl.blogspot.com).

Steve is married to Toni Lindahl, a pastel artist. They currently reside in North Carolina. They have two adult children, Nicole and Erik, and one grandchild, Ava.

Website: http://www.stevelindahl.com/

Blog: http://stevelindahl.blogspot.com/

Facebook: https://www.facebook.com/steve.lindahl.3

Instagram: https://www.instagram.com/stevelindahlwriter/ (@stevelindahlwriter)

Twitter: https://twitter.com/lindahlst (@lindahlst)

Amazon author page: https://www.amazon.com/Steve-Lindahl/e/B0031GLA5Y/ref=sr_ntt_srch_lnk_1?qid=1512223939&sr=8-1

Goodreads author page:
https://www.goodreads.com/author/show/3117087.Steve_Lindahl

Other Books by Steve Lindahl

Hopatcong Vision Quest

Blurb:
Two drownings occur in Lake Hopatcong within days of each other, with similar circumstances. Diane is certain the deaths of her mother and of Ryan's wife were not accidents, despite the results of the official investigation. What she doesn't suspect is that the trail to the justice she seeks runs through a past life she and her friends shared hundreds of years earlier. With the help of a hypnotist, Diane, Ryan, and Martha look into their hidden memories. They learn that they lived in a Native American village on the shores of the waters that later became the lake they love.

Oota Dabun, Diane's counterpart in her past life, always dreamed of having a vision quest, a rite normally reserved for the young men of her village. This Lenape woman reaches for her dream in an unusual and compassionate fashion which teaches Diane a great deal about the capacity of the soul they share. Diane discovers relationships as well as repeating events, both of which provide clues that might lead to the justice she's after. Along the way she learns about life, love and the strength of the human soul.

Link:
https://www.amazon.com/Hopatcong-Vision-Quest-Steve-Lindahl-ebook/dp/B01M1O6NG1

Under a Warped Cross

Blurb:
A thrilling adventure set in medieval Ireland, Britannia, and Scandinavia, *Under a Warped Cross* tells the story of

Abigail, Goda, and Waso, three siblings raised in the home of an Anglo-Saxon hog farmer. The medieval Catholic church is struggling to overcome pagan beliefs still prevalent in Britannia, so when Abigail, the youngest of the three, is wrongly accused of incest, the priests make an example of her. This tragic event changes all their lives as Goda and Abigail run off together and Waso begins a quest to find them.

Along with Waso, Goda, and Abigail, the novel follows the life of a young, Persian woman, Stateira, who has led a hard life since she was sold by her father. The story also tells of Jolenta, whose life experiences have motivated her to help victims of church abuse, a former monk, Elfgar, who works with Jolenta when he's sober, and Duette, Jolenta's daughter, who has reached the age where she must make decisions about the direction of her life.

Under a Warped Cross paints a picture of life in the middle ages within a plot filled with fury, sin, and violence, but also love, determination, and strength.

Link:
https://www.amazon.com/Under-Warped-Cross-Steve-Lindahl-ebook/dp/B07BB3G3QY

Chasing Margie

Blurb:
Howard and Emma Gladstone are at their summer lake house in the early twentieth century, when their daughter, Margie, disappears. The police suspect she's been kidnapped, but there is no ransom note. Despite an enormous effort on land and underwater, no sign of Margie is found. Yet the search continues, pursued at first by Howard then by his descendants.

Ninety-five years later, in 2018, Sarah Duncan meets a woman who claims to have discovered DNA evidence indicating Sarah is descended from the missing Margie Gladstone. Sarah is a lower-middle-class, thirty-year-old woman, who lives paycheck to paycheck. Her life consists primarily of working at a clothing store and taking care of her senile mother. Could she obtain a small portion of the Gladstone fortune? What would the money mean to the quality of her life? How can she find out if any of this is possible? And most importantly—what happened to Margie?

Chasing Margie: A case that wouldn't stay cold is set at Lake Hopatcong, NJ, and in New York, spanning the years from 1923 to 2019.

Link:
https://www.amazon.com/Chasing-Margie-Case-That-Wouldnt-ebook/dp/B08XQVVXFJ

Made in the USA
Middletown, DE
07 August 2022

70339540R00129